The Journey of Velvet Brown

Also by Myra King and published by Ginninderra Press
*City Paddock*

Myra King

# The Journey
# of Velvet Brown

*The Journey of Velvet Brown*
ISBN 978 1 76041 036 0
Copyright © Myra King 2015
Cover: Martin Gerritsen

First published 2015 by
**GINNINDERRA PRESS**
PO Box 3461 Port Adelaide 5015
www.ginninderrapress.com.au

Monsters are real. They live inside us, and sometimes, they win.

Stephen King

**1**

## Journal: Friday 11 January

I'm writing this down because Kaleen said I should, in case anything happens to me. She can be a bit dramatic sometimes. I think it's because she's a crime writer. She has this amazing imagination when it comes to working out convoluted plots and scenes, but she blurs fiction with reality. If she was reading this, she'd be laughing now and telling me that my reality is like fiction, fantasy even, but I know, and she knows, it's not. I've been right about the monsters too many times for her to doubt it.

I see monsters. I'm like the boy in that famous movie who sees dead people when nobody else can, except I'm a fourteen-year-old girl and I see monsters when nobody else does.

At first, I didn't even know they were monsters. I had no comparison for scary, which is synonymous with monsters, I guess, except for the picture books I had when I was little. But my monsters aren't anything like those. Or the fairy tale ones.

Kaleen Pingelly's my best friend and the only one I trust to tell. We've grown up next door to each other from when we were both four years old. 'Next door' is a relative term, as we live in farmhouses four kilometres apart, although most of those kilometres are on her side of the fence. Our property is small, but large enough for Dad's six prize merino sheep. And my pet goat, Sebby.

Kaleen has a theory about what I see in certain people. The monsters. She says it's sort of their aura energies showing through them, revealing the real shape of what and who they are. Their true characters.

Seeing monsters is scary and startling, but it's useful at times. Picture this. You rock up at school one morning and find all the kids ahuddle in whisper and conspiracy. The boys especially are buzzing. Across the car park their focus becomes visible. Today we have a relief teacher. Her back is to you as she bends to take some folders from the back seat of her car. But the golden swing of long hair promises gorgeousness and gasp.

She strides towards your classroom. The girls are jealous, the boys rapturous. Only you are unmoved. You've seen her hidden face. Category two monster. And so, while the others learn the hard way that beauty, youth and female do not automatically mean pushover, you've been in best behaviour and avoided time out, or worse.

My fourteenth birthday came up last year, on New Year's Eve. When I was younger, I used to think all those fireworks were put on for me. I soon learned they weren't. I've never felt special since, only different.

I'd already worked out what my New Year's resolution would be. Helping Kaleen with this ability of mine. She's not only a top friend but, as I said, she's an awesome writer. Already written a novel. Finished it a month ago and now she's looking for a publisher, hoping her age will give her the advantage, a bit of a spin for the publisher to market her on. It's a great book too. Crooks and coppers, that sort of stuff. She said it's literary as well, but mostly crime, as the crime genre sells better. She knows tons about writing and she's won heaps of prizes.

Because of her age, she's not eligible for most writing competitions, so she's had to enter stories in her sister's name. Her sister, Coral Lee, is eighteen. One time, Coral Lee stole Kaleen's prize money. I'd told Kaleen before not to trust her. Coral Lee was supposed to put it in the bank, but she spent it on her dozy boyfriend, Dwayne. The latest iPhone. The thing is, Coral Lee has had the look of a Category Three monster, ever since she's been going out with Dwayne. They say love can drive you crazy and now I believe it.

I've been helping Kaleen check out publishers for her book. I've already proofread her manuscript. If we arrange a meeting with them, I can see if they are monsters or not, and if they are, what kind. My gift of seeing monsters in people does not extend to photos or pictures.

Anyway, there is really only one very bad monster type you need to be careful of. The Up Your Own Arse monster. Category one. The colour of a thunderstorm, it has jagged black edges, leading into crevices which are depthless, especially about the eyes, which are inevitably of purple hue. Around its lips, the lines droop down in perpetual petulance…

I hear a noise and jump. Kaleen is standing behind me.

'Gee, Vel,' she says, 'you can't put those words together – perpetual petulance. Really bad alliteration. That's when you have words starting with the same letter and…'

'I know what alliteration is, Kaleen. I do English lit., too,' I say.

Kaleen always calls me Vel, short for Velvet. I don't call Kaleen Kay, as her parents won't have it. Same with Coral Lee: woe betide (that's Shakespeare) anyone who calls her Coral and not Coral Lee. I think it's a bit silly really and so does Kaleen. But you can't pick your parentals, can you?

Another thing which bothers me is that Kaleen just walks into my house without knocking. But if I did that in her house and her mother found out, I'd be banned. Or Kaleen would be grounded for having such a rude friend.

'How long have you been standing there?' I smack-shut my laptop.

'And you don't need inevitably. Sounds clunky.'

Kaleen reaches down and tries to open my laptop. I keep my hand over it, keeping it closed.

Kaleen looks fuzzy today and I hope to god she's not turning into a monster. That can happen: people you've known for ages can morph overnight, especially at our stage of life, puberty. Kaleen almost did go into Category Two once, the Angry at the Drop of a Rat monster, when Mr Hanker, or Hanker Wanker, as we all call him at school, picked on her for not doing PE. Hanker Wanker is definitely an Up Your Own Arse Category One monster. More fussy than us teenagers in the fashion stakes, he's forever peering and preening himself in the classroom window's reflection. Even has a comb in his top pocket. What makes Category One so dangerous is they only think of themselves. And evil lurks where empathy doesn't.

'Okay,' I say. 'I'll fix it later. What's up with you?'

Kaleen looks startled. 'What do you mean, Vel? Do I look funny?'

'No, just sort of vibratory.'

Her shoulders loosen and she rolls the spare chair over to my desk. 'That's okay then. I am a bit excited actually. I've got an awesome angle for my next book.'

'Geez, Kaleen, let's get *Bitter the Taste of Murder* out of the way first. You know, you really ought to change that title. I'm sure the last publisher I sent your manuscript to didn't read any of it. I mean, his reply was back within two minutes of me sending. Couldn't possibly have read even the synopsis in that time.'

Kaleen furrows her brow and sniffs. 'I wonder if I should shorten it. I really don't think it summarises it very well. I hate doing synopses.'

I was nearly going to say 'You've only done one', but Kaleen is leaning forward in that pose which says, 'I have something to tell you and I need you to listen. Now.'

I swivel my chair around to face her.

'Actually, Vel,' she says, lifting her lips upwards in a faint smile, 'I think I'll wait, see if you can work it out for yourself. Test that ability of yours.'

I frown and then smile too. It's hard to stay mad at Kaleen for long. 'Okay, but you've got to give me some clues. Someone, or something, I can go on.'

'Don't worry, Vel. You'll know soon enough. Anyway, have you ever thought of becoming a writer yourself? What you've written is pretty good really. And with a name like Velvet Brown, you'd have it made.'

I drum a beat on my laptop and laugh.

Kaleen stretches her arms behind her head, fingers interlocked. For a second, her face shades over blue. I'm about to ask her what's wrong, when suddenly she sits up straight.

'Have to go,' she says, getting up and nearly knocking over the chair. 'Mother has a dinner party on tonight. You're invited, by the way.'

I shake my head.

Kaleen grabs my hand. 'Please say you'll come. Mother's counting on it. Father has invited the foreman from his company. And our head stockman. I think Mother wants moral support. She's even invited her gardener.'

I know instantly what she means. The Pingellys are what the British call Old Money. Or what my Mum would call bloody posh. Kaleen's mother would want me and the gardener to be there to make it look like they don't mind rubbing hands or sharing meals with ordinary people. Must be something heavy going on at Kaleen's father's work. Not only does he run their cattle and sheep station but he also owns a manufacturing business making car parts for all over the world.

As if reading my mind, Kaleen says, 'The workers are on strike. Don't know what it's all about, really, except Father's been in a shirty mood all week.'

That's another difference between Kaleen and me. She hybridises swearwords, shirty for shitty, heck for hell, frick for… Well, you know.

Me, I usually don't hold back. Different upbringing, I guess.


Mum's working shift tonight so I ask Dad if it's okay for me to go to the dinner party. He inherited the walkabout gene (my great-grandmother was Indigenous) and he's between jobs at the moment, sort of a house-husband or, as he put on the census the other day, a shepherd. I wonder if six sheep, even if they are prize merinos, constitute a flock.

I get to Kaleen's early and her mother directs me upstairs to Kaleen's room. From her window I see the gardener, Jim, heading out to his workman's cottage at the far end of the Pingellys' huge garden. He's a funny-looking arrangement, lank hair tied back seventies-style, and in all the years I've known Kaleen, he's always been in overalls and this oversized floppy hat. I can see another guy standing near his door. Blue singlet. Stubby shorts. Neck to toe tatts visible from here. He's got that expectant look of a wife welcoming home her husband.

'Who's the Hells Angel, Kaleen?' I say, as Kaleen emerges from the shower.

Rubbing her hair in a towel, she looks out over my shoulder. 'Oh, that's the new foreman. I met him last week when he came here for talks with Father. He's the union rep as well. Looks pretty gnarly, hey?'

'Gnarly? I wouldn't call him that.'

'Gnarly is also old biker's lingo, Vel. I've been reading stuff about them. Do you know what getting their Red Wings means?'

I did, but I wasn't going to say so. I was curious to see where this was going. 'Kaleen, you mean to say he really is a bikie?'

Kaleen's voice slows, like someone speaking to a foreigner. 'No, Vel. I said, that's the foreman from Father's work, they all call him Chocka. The gardener used to be a bikie, though. He's got tatts too, mostly on his arms. Can't see them with his overalls on.'

I draw back from the window and sit down on Kaleen's bed. 'I don't like the look of him.'

Kaleen's favourite clown doll falls down from the shelf above our heads, and we both jump.

Kaleen looks at me, her eyes squinting, almost shut. 'Is he a monster then? I thought so. Can you see anything monstery from here?'

'Only his tatts,' I retort.

Kaleen opens her eyes. 'No, heck, Vel. Not Chocka. I meant the gardener.'

I'm glad she said heck. If she'd said hell, it would have rhymed with Vel and I wouldn't have been able to stop myself from laughing. She wouldn't have appreciated that. I can see she is deathly serious. And I wonder if this is anything to do with what she wouldn't tell me this afternoon, about her new idea for another crime novel.

At dinner, the transformation of the two men is nothing short of amazing. Really, they're overdressed for what looks to be a casual dinner party. I saw the table setting. Both have suits on, there's not a tatt, or oversized floppy hat in sight, their hair's combed back and their shoes gleam. Reminds me of old Hanker Wanker. The foreman's suit appears to be a better cut. Hanging around posh people, like the Pingellys, teaches you to notice things like that. How the lapels are cut, the type of stitching and that sort of stuff. They're both super polite and not bad at using their cutlery, although I see that Jim, the gardener, uses his steak knife to butter his bread roll.

It's the first time I've seen the head stockman too. No one seems to work for Mr Pingelly for long. The stockman's dressed in full cowboy get up. And whistle-stop clean. Even his hat, sitting on an empty chair beside him, looks freshly laundered.

If Kaleen's mother had been nervous, she isn't showing it now. She ignores the stockman and turns to the foreman. 'So, Chucky is it?' she says, holding up an eyebrow like she does her little finger when drinking tea.

Chocka puts down his soup spoon and smiles. 'Chocka, Mrs Pingelly. Chocka. It's easier to remember than my given name. My parents are from Croatia. My full name is Concertichocka Saltarelli.'

Kaleen's mother lowers her eyebrow and goes back to eating her meal.

I start scooping the soup away from the middle like I see her doing.

'So, what did your parents do in Croatia, Chocka?' Kaleen's father asks.

I'm not surprised he doesn't know. Chocka's probably not been working for him for long either.

Jim hunches forward, almost dropping his spoon into his bowl. Kaleen stares at him and then at Chocka.

Chocka glances at the gardener and then his face becomes passive. 'They were into security,' he says. 'Had their own business, actually.' Then he darts a strange look at Kaleen.

I scan around to see if anyone else notices, but they're all heads-bent over their soup. I can't wait to talk to Kaleen. I'm wishing this meal was over. I'm seeing lots more than their words. And I'm really surprised at what I see.

Luckily there are only four courses and Kaleen asks if we can be excused after the cheese. So different in our house: even if we have company, we often balance trays on our laps, in front of the TV. And get up when we want.

Soon we're in her room, with the door shut. My breath comes rushing out and my words are muddled.

Kaleen puts up her hand like someone answering a question at school. 'Don't say anything, Vel. Tell me tomorrow. Go home and think about it. Although I am dying to know what you saw.'

My 'sight' has changed over the years, sort of grown with me. Just like a muscle you've exercised, or a piece of music you've practised over and over, it's strengthened, I suppose. The monsters have modified. And the colours I see around most people, especially non-monsters, change with their moods. Blue for sad, yellow for happy, red for anger, that sort of thing.

I've read about how some people see auras around others. Can even tell if those people are sick, or healthy. But when I meet someone for the first time who turns out to be a monster, they have this fuzzy outline, you know, like a badly printed newspaper page, where you blink, wondering if you have something in your eyes. Then it clears to one of what I've figured out over the years are four categories.

Coral Lee, Kaleen's sister, is not what I'd term a real Category Three, which I call an Away in the Clouds monster, but she has her moments. Like just before she stole Kaleen's prize money. A Category Four monster, Head in the Sand, is not a bad sort at all, mostly a bit timid. If you have to meet a monster, it's the best of the four by far. Although you do have to watch your back: its cowardly nature tends to make it switch sides. Dad and my brother Danny are mild Category Fours. A Category Two, Angry at the Drop of a Rat monster, is pretty scary, but most times full of bluff. Category one? Well, like I've said, that's another matter entirely.

**2**

The next day is Saturday and even though I set the alarm for nine, I'm awake at eight. I can't wait to see Kaleen. Apart from telling her what I saw at the dinner party, I've also got some good news. When I got home last night, I had this email from a Canadian publisher who seems really interested in *Bitter the Taste of Murder*. I'm not sure how I'll be able to check him out monster-wise if we can't meet him in the flesh, so to speak. But it is encouraging.

A strong wind blows the peach tree branch against my window like someone trying to get in. I can hear Sebby bleating feed-me protests from his yard.

There's no way I can go to the Pingellys' before ten. They breakfast in the conservatory around nine on weekends. As it turns out, though, Mum bangs on my door at eight-thirty.

'Vel, can you come down? Don't worry about getting dressed. Just put on your dressing gown.' Her voice sounds strained, like the time Dad upended the tractor into the barbed wire fence.

Two policewomen are waiting for me as I descend the stairs.

The taller one stretches out her hand. 'You must be Velvet? What a great name.' Her mouth is smiling, but her eyes look tired.

I think to myself, Wait until Kaleen hears about this. One of her detectives in *Bitter the Taste of Murder* is a woman.

'I'm Detective Anne Finley and this is Constable Sarah Roberts.'

The other policewoman takes my hand briefly. A short shake. It reminds me of what I saw when Kaleen dared me to sneak a peek into the boys' toilets. Looking at her face, I feel a cold sensation going up my body by degrees, a bit like when you walk slowly out into the ocean instead of plunging right in.

'When last did you see Kaleen Pingelly?'

I shiver and pull my dressing gown tightly around me. Kaleen Pingelly, like they needed to tack on her surname so I'd make no mistake who they meant.

After they leave, I sit staring into the TV even though it's not on. I can't get my head around their words. It's like they were speaking another language.

Kaleen is missing. Her towel, her watch, and her riding boots had been found near the river. The alarm was raised when her horse, Watson, returned to the stables without her. That had been before seven. And still no sign. They'd also found her iPhone, and her last unsent message was to me.

I can hear Mum on the phone in the other room, her voice in low whispers, but what she says carries louder than a shout. 'Yes, it's terrible, Margery. Poor girl has probably drowned…undercurrent… Yes, and those tree roots…'

There seems to be something I'm not getting. What would Kaleen think of all this? My stomach and fists clench and I feel bile burning my throat.

Mum doesn't stop me when I cycle out, just tells me to be careful and be home at lunchtime so that she won't worry. I can't meet her eyes. I know what I'll see there and I'm not ready for that. Some things you don't want to know.

While I'm cycling, it's like I can hear Kaleen's voice in my head. I relive the evening before. Those men, what I know about them. The monsters I saw. And I swear out loud, 'Bloody hell. Bloody hell!' As the words echo, I laugh when I think what Kaleen would have said instead. So I yell, 'Blurry heck, blurry heck' like that will incant her back.

Then I start crying so hard the road ahead is a blur with my tears. Why didn't I insist on telling her what I saw? A Category One monster, definitely, and that was the most surprising. But that other one? I'd been puzzling about him most of the night, waking every few hours. What had I seen? Something without category, for sure, but strangely familiar? I pedal harder and drag my hand across my eyes, clearing my vision.

A search and rescue helicopter hovers above me and whirrs to where I see the river snaking around the bend. Reeds sway against the wind and even the ducks appear to be gone. Ahead, a roadblock holds me back from getting any closer. I stow my bike in some bushes. I figure with such a police presence it should be safe enough. I search out our little goat track and find my way to where we usually go swimming. It's upwind to the flow and nowhere near where the police seem to be searching. I can see several of them in the distance downstream, scuffling through the scrub. And a boat with scuba divers slipping from it into the murky water.

Waves of mismatched current slap against the riverbanks, and flotsam made of branches and rubbish swirls past me. A newspaper, wind-bent, sweeps along and curls itself around a sapling sucking water from the river's mud. The paper's so close to my hand I find myself catching it instinctively. To stop it flapping and drawing unwanted attention, I slip behind a huge river gum. The wind ignores me here. I slump against the tree's broad base, and the paper collapses like a sail in a becalmed sea.

I close my eyes, take a deep breath. What would Kaleen want me to do? I can't believe she went swimming. She's not a fool. Michael Foggarter, the school's swimming champion, had been taken by the river, in full swell like this, only a year back. And I can't believe she would leave her watch on the river bank. She wouldn't have worn it at all, if she knew she was going there to swim. I was with her when she won the bid on eBay for that watch. She was so excited. An antique. From Torquay, Devon, where Agatha Christie was born.

Look for clues. I hear Kaleen's voice again. I open my eyes and see the paper still clutched in my hands. It's yesterday's *News*, and the headlines are all politics. I start to scrunch it up, but a breeze curves itself around the trunk and tugs open a page. There's a headline on that page too: 'Small Parts Auto Strike Reaches Stalemate Talks Are Continuing'. In a photo, Kaleen's father is standing in front of a production line. The foreman, Chocka, is behind him, his face and arms folded.

There's also a short unrelated column in the bottom left-hand corner under a smaller headline: 'Bikie Gang Unrest'. It's about rival gangs from all around Australia encroaching on each other's territory. Apparently it's invited intrusion. Delegated killings paid for by high-profile people. Heads of companies, politicians. Anyone who can afford the fee, but not the dirt. There's a close-up picture of the Jugular Jackals' Colours. Those of the local bikie gang. Colours are the different mandatory logos adorning every biker's leather-jacketed back. This one was a black jackal's head, knife gritted between its teeth, red eyes lolling, set in a divided halo of green and orange.

A muscle and leather-bound member, titled the Annihilator, with his Harley Davidson clamped between his thighs, squeezes into another photo. His face has been blanked out. I wonder just who the press are protecting. I gasp and start shaking when I see the red-penned circle above his head, like a cartoon bubble, and the words written in it. For I know, as sure as sunlight, that it's Kaleen's writing.

I peer closely at the scribble blurred from the river spray; I read out the words: 'turn to page thirty-four'. The paper's too thin to have that many pages; most of it's blown away. I scan down to where it's come from and for a few moments contemplate calling out to the police. Almost as quickly, I decide not to. How can I explain anything?

Back at home I check out our recycle bin, find yesterday's paper and turn to page thirty-four. I'm not expecting to find anything, no red-inked circle of words. It turns out I don't need them. Page thirty-four is taken up with pictures of a garden. The Pingellys' garden, in all its gloriousness of hibiscus and agapanthus and sweeping lawns, defying last year's drought. And, standing in almost the same pose as Kaleen's father did in the other photo, is Jim, his face set like a slapped arse. The article is all about the upcoming Open Garden party Kaleen's mother is having this Sunday. Money to be raised for Pool Safety Awareness.

I think of our English lit. teacher, what she said about irony. I also recall those rules I've heard sung so many times in that safety advert: Shut the pool gate. Learn to swim. And the one that keeps repeating, Watch your mate. I swallow hard. Feel the tears prickling my throat again.

There's an interview with Kaleen's mother about how much the garden means to her. How it's the salvation of her sanity. And that she couldn't have kept it up without her faithful gardener, Jim. Also about how far back the garden goes, long before they bought the farm, and how it was made famous by its former owner, an English landscaper. Is this what Kaleen was trying to tell me about? The garden?

When I get to Kaleen's, everything seems deserted, except the marquees being erected for the garden party. I can see Jim helping, giving directions to the workmen, who are struggling against the wind. The show must go on. Or more likely no one has thought to cancel it yet. I see Watson looking expectantly over the rails of his paddock. I toss him some fallen apples as I sneak through the orchard. Then I slide along the wooden paling fence to the gardener's cottage.

My mind is whirring like the helicopter. Perhaps I'm wrong this time about the monsters I saw. There is always a first for everything.

I think about Chocka. What was his real name again? Who could remember that? And if they find that Kaleen didn't drown in the river and she and he went missing, everyone would say they just knew him as Chocka. How could he be traced? He would be almost as good as nameless. And his family had a security business? Oh, god, I whisper, as I recall his last name sounded more Italian than Croatian. It ended in 'i', a dead giveaway.

I start to shake again and press myself against the cold stone wall of the gardener's cottage. Some old bricks make up a precarious balance for me to reach the window. I swipe away the dust and cobwebs, and peer inside. I nearly topple backwards when I see who is lying on the bed. When I tap on the window, she turns over and sits up, rubbing her eyes and yawning.

'Kaleen,' I mouth, and see her hurry to the door. I check briefly before entering, but no one can see me from this angle, except perhaps from the house. I'd seen Kaleen's mother at the river, but her father had been nowhere in sight. I'm hoping he's not home.

I pull the door shut behind me and lean against it, breathing heavily. 'Christ, Kaleen. What the hell have you done?' my voice hisses, but I'm not waiting for an answer, 'Half the town is looking for you. Search and rescue, the lot.'

'Listen Vel, you won't believe what I've found out –' Kaleen stops mid-sentence, her words slide up. 'Search and rescue?'

I don't know whether to hug her or hit her. I feel my fist clenching, but I drop it to my side. 'You don't know, do you?' I say.

Kaleen sits down on the bed and pulls on a sneaker. She's frowning and going red. 'Well, I didn't mean to fall asleep. I was awake most of the night and I've been up since five.' She ties her shoelace, fumbling with the knot. 'Like, I can explain everything if you give me a chance.'

'No, Kaleen. Not now. You've got to get down to the river and let them know you're okay. My bike's on the other side of the orchard. Take that, it'll be quicker. Or you could get Jim to phone your mum.'

Kaleen shudders. 'No thanks. Listen, Vel, can I borrow your hoody?'

I start to ask why, but Kaleen has the look of a marathon runner in the last few yards of her race.

The river is about four kilometres from Kaleen's place. I get there and find my bike not far from the roadblock. I start to imagine what their faces would have been like when Kaleen turned up. Gee, she'd have a lot of explaining to do. I decide not to add to her embarrassment. I'll see her later.

I'm halfway home when an ambulance, a blur of white and flashing lights, screams past me, spitting up gravel. I pedal faster, glad the wind seems to have dropped.

When I get home, Mum meets me at the gate. 'Velvet, darling. It's all okay. Kaleen's been found. She's in the hospital. But she'll be fine. Aren't you cold with just your T-shirt on?'

I'm seriously wondering if being friends with Kaleen is good for my health. My heart's beating a tattoo louder than any of those on Chocka.

**3**

The next day, I arrive at the hospital. Kaleen is sitting up in bed with her laptop on her meals tray. She's looking suitably pale, but I can tell she's enjoying all the attention.

Before I can speak, she grabs my hand. 'Do you know, Vel, I've been reading about how Agatha Christie went missing. No one knew where she was for ages. She got heaps of publicity over it. Maybe I should have hidden out for a while.'

'Bloody hell, Kaleen, you can't be serious.' I sound angrier than I feel. Actually, I'm a bit relieved. I had been thinking she might have done it all on purpose. That damn book of hers.

Kaleen clears her throat and draws the sheet up to her chin. 'What do you want to hear first? Before you found me, or after?'

I sigh. 'Well, I've guessed a lot of the after already. I suppose you got into the river and they rescued you.'

'It was awesome, actually, Vel. Way exciting. No one noticed me on your bike with your hoody on, so I snuck through the bush, stripped off and went in upriver, at our usual spot. The wind and the river had gone down and the flow was fine. I knew I'd be okay. And I even managed to scrape my legs against a submerged log. Added to the authenticity.' Kaleen lowers her voice. 'Then I made my way up the bank on the other side and crawled along in the reeds. They found me not long after that.'

'Hell, Kaleen, have you got any idea how crazy I've been going? And your poor mother, she would have been out of her mind.'

Kaleen puts a finger to her mouth. 'Will you shut up a bit? Someone might hear you. And I'm supposed to be resting.'

I start to get up. Kaleen grabs my arm, but I pull away. 'You don't get it, Kaleen. This is not fiction. People have given up their time, searching.

And those scuba divers and the people on the boat put themselves in danger.'

'Don't be so uptight, Vel. I made their day when they found me. Another successful rescue. Some of them may even get bravery awards.'

I realise it's like talking to Sebby. I sit back on the visitor's chair and fold my arms.

Kaleen lowers her eyelids. 'Look,' she says, 'it's like this. I had all those clues you wanted ready yesterday morning. I even had a message already keyed into my iPhone, to send to you, to come and meet me here. I was putting out the last clue, the newspaper, by the river when the blurry wind started, blew it up in the air and it spooked Watson. He got loose, bolted off and I ran after him. That's why my stuff was left there.'

I unfold my arms and say slowly, 'So, I was right about the garden party pic being a clue. Not sure how the bikies fit in, though. And the watch, Kaleen? Was that a clue too?'

Kaleen grimaces. 'Symbolising time will tell and all that? I didn't mean to leave it, or anything, there. I was going to be with you when you were doing the solving. But I forgot everything when I was trying to catch Watson. I even dropped my iPhone. He kept stopping and when I'd nearly get to him, he'd take off again. By the time I gave up, I was more than halfway home, so I thought, What the heck, I may as well check something out.' Kaleen pauses and looks me in the eyes. 'I've had my suspicions about Jim, the gardener.'

'Me too,' I say, nodding.

'Well, apart from other things, I thought he'd been having it off with Mother.'

I'm not prepared for this. 'What? Like the English say, she's having a bit of rough?'

I can see Kaleen turning the colour of embarrassment, sort of puce. 'Yes,' she says. 'Thankfully, I was wrong. When I was almost home, I heard someone coming. It was Donovan.'

'Who's Donovan?'

'The head stockman. Donovan O'Reilly.'

I rub my chin. 'I don't think he talked at all at the dinner party. I never got to hear his name.'

'Yeah,' Kaleen says. 'He's the quiet brooding type. Comes with the saddle.'

I cock my head. 'So he was coming? Looking for you?'

'No.' Kaleen goes a darker puce. There's a long pause before she starts talking. 'I mean, he was coming. You know. Coming. I was right about Mother playing up, but I had the wrong guy. They were in the bushes not four metres away from me. I could hear Mother's voice, well, you know.'

Once again, Kaleen goes quiet. It's the first time I've ever known her to be lost for words.

I try to find them for her by changing the subject. 'So how did you end up in the gardener's cottage? I would have thought he'd be up really early with the open day and everything.'

'That's what I thought, too. So after I saw that someone had already put Watson in his paddock, I crept over to the cottage. Jim wasn't there. But it was open. I went in thinking I might as well look around anyway. I still wasn't convinced about the guy. Then, when I heard sounds, I hid in the bedroom.' Kaleen takes a sip of water from her glass on the bedside cabinet. 'He and Chocka had come back. Chocka must have slept over. Chocka was talking about the strike. As I told you before, Vel, he's also the union rep. He was telling Jim that Father was going to get workers from outside, to break up the strike. Scab labourers, he called them. And all the real workers want is a fair deal. Better pay. I know Father pays awfully lousy wages.'

'I'm not surprised,' I say.

Kaleen looks at me again, her eyes bright. 'And I don't blame Mother. Donovan's hot. I'm just glad it's not the gardener. Hey, Vel, what you said before, about Mother being worried sick. You didn't say anything about Father. He wasn't looking for me, was he? He was probably off dealing with the scab workers, right?' Kaleen's face goes blank, no colour. But her voice is tight.

I know she doesn't really want to know. I rub her arm.

She smiles and continues. 'Anyway, I must have fallen asleep really deeply. I only woke up when you knocked on the window. There was something else, too, Vel. Something Jim said.' Kaleen's breath is a visible blue. 'He's heard there's a contract out on Chocka. Fifteen thousand dollars. Jim found out from a member of the Jugular Jackals. An old friend of his.'

It's my turn to go quiet.

Then her tone brightens. 'On a different note, it must be early spring or something. Love and all that.'

As she says this I realise, in a flash of insight, what was familiar about the monster I saw in Chocka. The one I couldn't categorise. He was like Coral Lee. An almost monster. In crazy love. I suppose being male made him a little different.

'Don't say anything. Let me guess, Kaleen. Chocka and Jim are an item.'

Kaleen gasps. 'How did you know that? You're right. Chocka was calling the gardener Darling. Sort of *Brokeback Mountain* stuff. I think it's sweet. Although I don't know what he sees in the gardener.'

Kaleen shudders and just then the nurse pops her head in through the door and asks how we're doing, and says visiting time will be up in ten.

I look at Kaleen lying in her hospital bed, her face almost as white as the walls, and I know I'm not going to tell her that her father was the Category One monster I saw on the night of the dinner party. Anyway, he wasn't always that bad. But power can do that to people, change them. I think of the newspaper article. High profile people getting hit men from bikie gangs. And although I have a feeling I'm more surprised than Kaleen would be about her father, there are some things you know, you really don't want to know.

**4**

More about my ability before Kaleen gets here. She's due any minute – it's almost at the end of the school holidays and we don't want to waste any more time. I haven't seen her since she got out of hospital.

I've used up all my iPhone allowance, but she's been texting me. Kaleen said I should go over the monsters' main traits once more, just to get it clear in readers' minds, so here goes.

Category Four – AKA Head in the Sand Monster. Hates conflict. Changes sides for its own benefit. But if you have to meet a monster, one of the best, relatively speaking. Often they're actual relatives, as in Dad and my brother, Danny. Although they are modified versions.

Category Three – AKA Away in the Clouds Monster. Severe daydreamer, handles problems by denying them. Can say nasty things – has a knack of knowing what nasty things to say about the person that will hurt them the most. Kaleen's sister, Coral Lee, is an almost Category Three since she's been in love with her boyfriend, Dwayne.

Category Two – AKA Angry at the Drop of a Rat Monster. Pretty self-explanatory. Handles everything with extreme anger at the slightest provocation. Often red in an angularly distorted face, or has a fire-red aura.

Category One – AKA Up Your Own Arse Monster. Like our PE teacher, Hanker Wanker. Has a purple aura in jagged lines. Extremely vain. Loves itself exclusively. Lacks empathy. Very dangerous and…

A hand comes over my vision. I bring my head up sharply and swivel round.

Kaleen steps neatly aside and points at the screen. Her voice cuts over the low hum of my computer. 'What's the acronym stand for, Vel?'

I almost ask back 'What's an acronym?' and then remember it's the name of an abbreviation. The first letters of words. In this case AKA.

'Also Known As,' I say, frowning at her before continuing. 'Can't you at least make some noise when you come in? Scared the shit out of me.'

'I'm trying something out.'

'Don't tell me. You're getting into character for your next book.'

Kaleen flops into the spare chair, her black-brown hair hanging down around her face. 'How did you know that? Are you becoming psychic as well now? Anyway, I'm glad to see you working on this.' She waves at the screen. 'When you've finished writing it all, we'll print it out and bury it in a time capsule or something.'

I rub my eyes. 'No one would believe it.'

'That's my point. It's bound to be better understood in the future. Maybe lots of people will be able to do it. See monsters. Or you may pass the ability on to your kids.'

I groan, hit Save. And then click to open my emails. My computer tells me it won't let me in, that the server's having some sort of problem. I turn round to Kaleen.

She's looking down at her feet and shuffling them under the chair. I see she's barefoot, not even wearing socks.

'They say you're quieter without shoes and noisy clothes,' she says, still looking down.

'Noisy clothes?'

Kaleen brings her eyes directly to mine. I can see the flecks of gold in the irises. Strange that I hadn't noticed those before.

'You know, Vel, like that pink dress you wore when you were a flower girl. It made a scratchy sound. You'd have had no hope sneaking up on anyone wearing that.'

'God, Kaleen, that was ages ago. I must have been about six.'

'That would be about right.' Kaleen leans over to my bedhead and drags down my clown doll (it's a twin to the one I gave her a few birthdays ago). She moves his arms and I can hear the rustle as the lace around his sleeve cuffs chafes his sides. She holds him up like an exhibit.

I take him from her and slide him back into his place, in the corner nook of the bedhead. 'That was your cousin's wedding, as I recall, Kaleen, and it was you who should have worn that revolting dress. I remember you talking me into doing it.'

'It didn't take much persuasion. Anyway, Vel, don't look so cross. I'm having a hard enough time as it is.'

I look at her again, and see her aura. It's a very faint but discernible blue. 'What's up?'

Kaleen sits down again and hooks a strand of hair behind her ear. 'Well, Jim's disappeared. Run off with Chocka, I think, 'cause they're both gone.'

I nod and we sit silently for a few minutes.

'Mother's going crazy trying to find a new gardener. She and Father had the most awful argument the other night. Father stormed off and didn't come back until morning. And Watson has laminitis. Mother had to call the vet, he was so sore.'

'Oh no, Kaleen. Is he okay now?'

'Yes, he is, we just have to keep him stabled and off the pasture. Can only let him out in the mornings and that's if it hasn't been frosty overnight. Something to do with too much sugar in the grass.'

I think about this for a moment. 'Laminitis. That's inflammation in the feet, isn't it?'

'Yeah, it can be bad if it's not treated. They go terribly lame.'

'Poor Watson. How are the other stock horses? And how's the hot stockman, Donovan?'

Kaleen goes from blue to pink, almost the same colour as the flower-girl dress. 'Try your emails again, Vel,' she says. 'You know I sent off those chapters of my book to the Canadian publisher, as he wanted. We've been emailing each other. Do you really think I ought to come up with another title?' Kaleen is always good at changing the subject.

An hour later, after taking some sugar-free mints to Watson and stroking the stock horses over the fence (they're having a day off), Kaleen and I end up in her office. Kaleen's house is huge, six bedrooms, three offices and two, as she calls them, drawing rooms. That's an English term for lounge rooms, apparently. Like being poorly instead of sick, and pudding instead of dessert. She doesn't have to have her computer in her bedroom like I do, although her bedroom certainly is big enough.

'Blast this server. I wonder what's going on?' She flicks her hair. 'Anyway, it doesn't matter, I've already printed out the emails.' Kaleen hands me a wad of papers.

'Crikey, Kaleen, what have you two been talking about? I haven't even checked him out yet. Don't get too friendly.'

Kaleen rolls her eyes, takes the papers from me, shuffles them and hands back eleven sheets. I scan through and read familiar stuff. It's some of her novel, *Bitter the Taste of Murder*.

'Okay, so you sent these?'

'I had to. He wanted the first two chapters, a synopsis and a blurb. You know, the bit you read on the back of a book, to see if it's any good.'

'I know what a blurb is.' I hadn't known, but I'm not going to tell Kaleen that.

Her hand goes up to her hair once more. And then I see it. Almost hidden, but ruffled to the surface, is a thick streak of white, like a skunk's stripe.

'Good god, Kaleen, what have you done to your hair?'

Kaleen grins. 'I thought you were never going to notice.'

She smiles again, then to my horror her smile fades, she gets up and turns her back on me. Her shoulders are shaking and I know she's crying. I gently pull her around, but she's already wiped her eyes with the back of her hand and now there's only the wet brightness to show there were any tears at all.

'It's not that bad, Kaleen,' I say, touching the offending lock. It feels different, a little more brittle than the rest of her hair.

'It's not that, Vel. It's everything. I mean, I've always known my parents don't care much about me, but now they've taken it to a new level. Mother would have never allowed me to do anything like this before. Gosh, I think she'd even let me get a tattoo now, if I asked.'

'Sounds like she's feeling guilty. Remember that episode in *The Simpsons*, when Marge and Homer were splitting up and Marge made extra treats for Lisa and Brat's, I mean Bart's, school lunches and…'

I stop. Kaleen has turned round again.

I walk over to the French doors just outside Kaleen's office. Through them I can see Mrs Pingelly and some old guy. He's got grey-brown hair and he's wearing blue jeans with faded denim patches on the knees. His sleeveless top shows tanned arms and surprisingly well developed biceps. Obviously he must be one of the new gardener hopefuls that Mrs Pingelly is interviewing for the job. Then I hear Watson neighing out. It's shrill and insistent.

'Kaleen, I think something's up.'

Kaleen comes over and stares out towards the stable block. Her face is dry. 'Watson's fine, Vel. He just doesn't like being shut away. That's all.'

Mrs Pingelly and her wannabe gardener pass so close I could have touched them if there wasn't glass between us. It's then I see his true self and shudder.

Kaleen looks at me and lifts an eyebrow, like her mother does. 'Okay, Vel, what type is he?'

I take a deep breath. 'Category two. Definitely Category Two.'

'Fudge, that's the angry rat one, isn't it? Oh goodness, just what I need. Blurry, blurry, heck.'

Now she reminds me of Flanders in *The Simpsons*, and how he won't swear, even when he's really upset. But I don't say anything. I've been working on my tact, another birthday New Year's resolution.

I do feel sorry for Kaleen, I really do. I mean, there are lots of times she brings stuff on herself. But none of what's been happening lately is her fault.

Watson calls out again, and now there's a different, longer, more urgent sound to it, like when one of the stock horses is left behind while the others are out droving and it's neighing for its mates.

Then, just behind the orchard, not far from the gardener's cottage, I see a white form. Definitely equine-shaped even though its head is down amongst the long grass at the bottom of the apple trees.

I grab Kaleen's arm. 'Look over there. None of your stock horses are white, are they?'

Kaleen answers in a flat sort of voice. 'Grey. You don't call horses white, even if they look white.'

She's still watching her mother and the Category Two. They're a long way away and the man appears almost normal, now that he's gone out of my monster-sight range, except for a red aura which trails behind him like a comet's tail. Mrs Pingelly is pointing to a clump of something that faintly shimmers in upright silvery plumes.

It's like Kaleen hasn't heard me. 'I'll have a word with Mother after he's gone. Not that she'll probably listen to me.'

I tug on her arm again. 'Kaleen,' I hiss, 'he's coming over to the stable block. Seems like he's loose.'

Kaleen half glances at me and then to where I'm pointing. 'Oh, for a minute I thought you were talking about the man.' She gives a half chuckle.

I smile. I'm pleased to be able to cheer her up, even if it's only a little.

'Probably a neighbour's horse,' she says, and heads outside. 'Mother wouldn't want it getting into her garden. We'd better catch it and then I'll ring around.'

The horse, a gelding, seems unconcerned as Kaleen slips a halter on it and leads it into the empty stall next to Watson's.

'Here you go, boy, some company for you,' she says to Watson.

She pulls open the top half of the stable door. The white horse sticks his head out immediately. It's then I notice he has the most strange-looking eyes. Blue as a winter sea, but with the outer rims in black, like mascara. Gorgeous, exotic-looking eyes.

'Hasn't he got the most amazing eyes, Kaleen? And his coat isn't really white at all, but cream.'

'He's a Cremello.' Kaleen chuckles again. 'Actually, it's okay to call Cremello horses white.'

'Cremello.' The name slips around my mouth like silk, and I know it's referring to his colour, not his breed. But I ask anyway. 'What sort is he? He doesn't look like your stock horses.'

Kaleen rubs the Cremello's nose. 'Well, he wouldn't. They're Walers. He looks like a Quarter horse.'

I've learned enough from Kaleen to know that Quarter horses have that name because they were bred in the USA to race over quarter miles. So I don't make any silly jokes.

Before I can ask more, Kaleen is heading me back to the house. As she approaches, the Category Two looks over. He pulls up a weed and bangs the dirt out on the lawn. He flashes a glimpse at us and grins. Hideous to me, but Kaleen smiles back, in reflex, I guess. Mrs Pingelly is watching him, her arms loosely folded.

'Sheesh,' Kaleen whispers. 'That looks like it's going well.'

We step back into her office. The computer pings up a new message. The server is still having problems.

'Who do you think owns him?'

'What?' Kaleen cocks her head. 'Oh, the horse? That's easy. He probably belongs to Old Ma Izzy, the Horse Lady. You've heard of Cat Ladies? Well, she's the equine equivalent. She'd have horses in the house if they made litter trays big enough for them. Nice old woman, though.'

'Izzy? Isobel?'

'No, her name's Rosalie Islington-Prior.'

'Sounds posh.'

'She moved here from the UK. About a year and a half ago. Bought the Jamisons' place. She sort of is a bit posh, but not snobby. Mother invites her to dinner sometimes. Great to talk to. Knows heaps about horses.'

I lean over and scratch the Cremello's neck. 'Better find out then. Do you have her number?'

'I do. Only thing is, if it's hers we'll have to take the horse there. She's like us, doesn't have a horse trailer.'

'The Jamisons' place is over the other side of the river, isn't it? That's a long way to walk, Kaleen. How will we get there?'

'Ride, of course. I'll lead the Cremello off Cody. You can take Donovan's horse, Ganny. He's that new one, but seems quiet.'

'Ganny?'

'Ganymede. I know, weird name, hey? That should tell you what Donovan's really like.' Kaleen's shoulders hunch up and she moves her feet. She's wearing her boots now and they make a scuffling sound. 'But don't ask, Vel. I don't want to talk about it.'

Ganny is a slender bay gelding with a curious distinctive blaze, like a huge white question mark on his face. Cody is shiny mirrored black and the youngest of their stock horses.

Kaleen rings Old Ma Izzy but gets no answer. She calls a few other numbers too, but no one's missing a Cremello horse.

'What are we going to do, Kaleen?'

'Go over there anyway. Izzy's probably outside. If the horse isn't hers, she's bound to know who it belongs to.'

We saddle up and when I'm aboard Kaleen gets me to hold the Cremello's lead rope. When she mounts, she takes it from me, directs him to the right side of her horse and holds both her reins in her left hand.

'We can't keep calling him the Cremello,' I say. 'How about Creamy?'

'Oh, very inspiring, that is.' Her voice is thick with sarcasm.

We ride on in silence, each of us coming up with up a new name. Shadow. The Phantom. Casper.

'Vel?'

'What?'

'Your turn.'

'I'm thinking.'

'Yes?'

'Well, Kaleen, he's blond, blue-eyed. Well built. What about Paul?'

'What? Who the heck is Paul?'

'Paul Newman. Gorgeous film star from the sixties. Mum buys his mayonnaise. He looks pretty good on the jar.'

Kaleen stares at me, wide-eyed. For a moment, I think she might even swear, but the moment passes as two kangaroos jump out in front of us. They bound in swift strokes easily clearing the ancient barbed-wire fence that is the Pingellys' farm boundary. As if on cue, a kookaburra laughs and lifts his grey and blue feathered form from a huge gum tree where he'd been perched.

Simultaneously, our horses spook sideways almost onto the road just as a truck is passing. Its brakes sound a squealing protest. Cody buckjumps and in one move Kaleen lets go of the Cremello's lead, gathers her reins and gets Cody's head up. The Cremello, lead rope hanging, stands perfectly still, faintly snorting in the direction of the departing truck. Then he relaxes and begins to eat the long grass. Cody and Ganny are still trembling.

'Look at that, Vel. Any other horse would have bolted off.'

I can see Kaleen's pretty impressed. I am too. I look at the Cremello. He's so beautiful. I feel an inner stirring. I've always wanted to have my own horse and never more than now. The yearning becomes a palpable ache in my stomach. Kaleen is so bloody lucky to have had horses all of her life. Mostly I can keep my envy to small letters, but it's screaming in capitals at the moment. Dad won't have a horse on our farm. Not enough land, and horses ruin fences. That's what he says when I ask or plead. I've given up now, after so many years.

I'm shaking too, from the wanting and a little fear, but I'm happy with myself for staying on, though. All those lessons in Kaleen's covered riding arena have paid off.

Without having to dismount, Kaleen leans over and manages to pick up the Cremello's lead rope. The streak of white hair falls out from beneath her riding hat. It reminds me of something.

'Lightning,' I say quietly.

'What? Lightning? Oh, gosh no, Vel, so unoriginal. A horse this good deserves something more. Anyway, we're never going to get there at this rate. Let's trot and if all goes well, are you up for a canter?'

I shorten my reins. 'As long as we don't get any more of those damn kangaroos.'

The rest of the ride is uneventful, but now there's a soft rain falling. Rubbish rain, my dad calls it. No good for wetting the grass but fine for getting you soaked.

A cloud squeezes out half a sun as we ride into Izzy's driveway. A huge, high-railed riding yard flanks a paint-poor weatherboard house. There are dogs barking, hidden from view, and several horses, tails aplume, dancing down a long paddock towards us. More horses, thoroughbreds and Shetlands and indistinguishable breeds in between, come to investigate, snorting and head tossing. The larger ones stretch sleek necks over the wooden rail fences. Somewhere unseen, I hear the unmistakable deep-throated neigh of a stallion. He sounds very large.

'God, Kaleen, you weren't joking. She is the Horse Lady.'

The Cremello still seems unperturbed. He pricks his ears and steps out neatly when Kaleen crosses over the path and opens the gate, near the cattle grid.

Ganny is unsure. He cocks his head, keeping an eye on the steel pipes, and almost slides me along the fence in his need to keep clear of them.

'Are you certain Ganny's a stock horse? He's not too sure about the grid.'

'I don't know much about him really. He came with Donovan. He's okay, isn't he? He seems pretty quiet, what I've seen of him anyway.'

There's a white-painted fence around the farm house. A Western saddle straddles it with a saddle blanket and bridle strewn across it. I see the bridle has no bit. But it's not a halter. Before I can ask Kaleen what type of bridle it is, a small truck glides up to the grid.

A woman sticks her head out. 'Helloo there, my good fellows,' she says.

It's several moments before I realise she's talking to the horses and not us. Seemingly satisfied that they're not going to spook, she drives the truck up alongside and pulls herself out. Bits of her seem to be dropping off until I see it's only hay, although I can't see any bales.

She closes the truck door softly. Drags a bag of what looks like horse pellets from the tray and without turning around, says, 'Now you would be Mrs Pine…Pinella's daughter. Let me think. Oh, I'm never good with the names.'

Kaleen slips in. 'I'm Kaleen, Mrs Islington-Prior. Mrs Pingelly's daughter.'

'Ah, grand so.'

Old Ma Izzy has a slight unaccountable accent. I find it calming and I'm betting the horses do too.

She touches Cody's shoulder. 'I do know who this fine gentleman is, though. It would be yourself, Cody, is it not, my good lad.' Once more she's talking to the horse.

Then she turns round and lays a long brown hand on Ganny's neck. Her grey hair flickers sunlight and there is a sparkle in her eyes that matches it. She's as far removed from a monster as you could possibly get. I feel Ganny relax beneath me.

'Well, then. But I haven't been meeting this dainty boy before today. And that's no lie.' She lifts her sparkling eyes to mine and stops. She stares at me for a long second and then nods like she's confirming something agreeable in her mind.

Kaleen sees the look and glances at me, both her eyebrows are up now like question marks. I give a slight shake of my head and Kaleen says nothing.

'So, lass, who is this fine gent? What would his name be for the calling?'

'Ganny,' I say.

'Ganymede,' chimes in Kaleen.

'Ah, yes, Ganymede.' Once more, Old Ma Izzy is addressing the horse. 'Nothing to fear, young man. Zeus is not here to abduct you.' She looks at me. 'Take him gentle, this boy. He'll mean you no harm, but that does not mean it will not be harm he's taking you to.'

She leans forward, traces Ganny's blaze mark with a forefinger and lifts Ganny's face to hers. She breathes out slowly into his nostrils as he is breathing in. It feels to me his very skin goes loose and then he gives an audible sigh. Relinquishing his breath with hers.

'Don't you girls be doing this, hear? Not with a horse you don't know.'

'We won't, Old Ma…Mrs Islington-Prior.' Kaleen's neck is colouring red up to her face. She lifts the lead rope and brings the Cremello around the other side of Cody into Old Ma Izzy's view. 'We just wanted to know, is this your horse? He was found wandering about our place this morning.'

Old Ma Izzy whistles softly. 'No, but more's the pity. What a beauteous spirit.'

Kaleen and I look at each other and grin. 'Spirit,' we both say in unison.

'So, Karla,' Old Ma Izzy touches my arm as she looks at Kaleen, 'Who is this lass?'

'She's my friend, Velvet, Velvet Brown.'

'Ah, that she would be. *National Velvet.*' Old Ma Izzy gives a chuckle. But then looks at me straight-faced. 'Welcome, lass, welcome.'

# 5

On the ride home, Kaleen seems to be sulking. 'What was that all about, Vel? All that welcome stuff and the way she looked at you. Like you were the messiah or something. And what did she mean about Ganymede and Zeus? Zeus is the Greek god of war, isn't he?'

I feel hilarity rising but it's swamped with those same questions that I'd been asking myself. Not the messiah part, though. Not that. My heart is held by the Aboriginal Dreamtime, or rather Dreaming, as it's not a time at all, but everything around us. This land, Australia.

'I think, Kaleen, that Ganymede was a mortal man, whom the gods fancied. They sent an eagle down to get him, or they turned him into an eagle. I can't remember which. I'd have to check up on the Net. That's if it's working yet. Tell me again why we can't just let the horses have their heads and get back quickly.'

As I knew it would, that got Kaleen off track, as she expounded for the umpteenth time why you shouldn't let horses gallop home. Especially touchy ones like Ganny as they're likely to bolt off, or start pulling, in their excitement to get back. She was ready to concede Ganymede was not as quiet as she'd first thought after we'd nearly ended up in a deep ditch. He had spooked again, this time at his own shadow.

Old Ma Izzy had offered to temporarily take care of the Cremello (whom we now called Spirit) at her place when she found the brand M, with a half circle around it, under his mane. She was fairly sure she knew who he belonged to. A Mr Marika, who bred Quarter horses and Arabs and lived not far from her. She said she'd get in touch with him as soon as she could. Apparently, she told us, as she sniffed loudly, he only checked his property on weekends. He had an overseer, who kept an eye on the horses in between.

The rain stops just as we are riding up into Kaleen's driveway. Watson screeches out a desperate neigh, like we'd been gone forever. And standing at the stock horses' paddock is Donovan, cowboy-hatted head tilted, water dripping from it, arms tightly folded. He's wearing full Western regalia, including riding chaps. He strides over and glares at Kaleen. His chaps make a scratchy rustling noise. Ganny snorts and jumps backwards. Strange, I think, seeing that he's Donovan's horse.

Still saying nothing, Donovan snatches Ganny's reins as I dismount.

Kaleen hands him Cody's reins too. 'They need a rub down and probably a drink. But let them cool off first,' she says to Donovan's departing back.

His shoulders hunch and we hear what sounds like a long string of words, spitted with Fs and Bs.

'He's peed off because we took his horse without asking.'

I shake rainwater from my jacket. 'Hell, Kaleen, I thought it was okay with him. We should've asked.'

'Should have, but didn't. He can't expect respect from me with what he's been doing with Mother.'

I stare for a long second at Kaleen; she's never acted like this before. Like a rich brat.

Then she looks over to the house. 'Sheet,' she hisses. 'Looks like the plain clothes are here again.'

'Plain clothes?'

'Yeah, you know, policemen. See, even their car is incognito.'

I see an unfamiliar white Holden parked parallel to the front door. White, the good guys' colour.

'I know what plain clothes policemen are, Kaleen,' I say, giving my jacket an extra shake.

'Well, they're a bit of disappointment, Vel. They just look like everyone else.'

'That's 'cause they're in civvies, Kaleen, you know, street clothes. They're not meant to stand out.'

'Yeah, but I was hoping I'd learn something for my new novel.'

'We have to get your first one off the ground, first,' I say. As Kaleen's agent of sorts, it sounds quite grand to say this and I feel myself smiling. 'Anyway, Kaleen, why are they here?'

She takes a deep breath. 'You remember all that trouble at Father's work? The scab workers. The strike.'

I nod, feel myself stiffen.

'Well, last week they came and took away his computers and all his paperwork. I guess they're bringing them back today.'

I change the subject. 'Gee, how about Spirit? He's one angel of a horse. I wonder if he's broken in.'

Kaleen is still glaring at the house. The front door opens and two men, of differing heights but still very tall, come out, flanking Mr Pingelly. He has his hands behind his back and for a moment I wonder if he's been handcuffed. But I sigh when I see him bring a hand around to scratch his nose. It's probably compliance he's trying to convey. His face is still that of a Category One. More jagged even, if that's possible.

As soon as we enter Kaleen's office, she screams like she's been bitten by a red back spider. 'Oh, no, they've taken my computer too.'

'Surely not. Why would they do that?'

Kaleen's scrabbling in the top drawer of her desk. She opens another and the contents tumble out in a confusion of pens, paper clips and staplers.

'My memory sticks. They're gone as well. And the one with *Bitter the Taste of Murder* on it. Why would they want that?'

It seems self-explanatory to me. But keeping with my tact resolution, I don't offer an answer. 'Don't worry,' I say. I go over to Kaleen, who has slumped onto the floor. She can be quite melodramatic at times. 'I have a copy, remember?'

Kaleen lies back, flings her arms in the air. 'I've done heaps of rewrites since I sent you that. So many changes.' She begins to sob.

A minute later Mrs Pingelly knocks on the office door. 'Are you girls all right in there? I have a phone call for you, Kaleen Joyce.'

The transformation in Kaleen is amazing. She jumps up, her voice almost normal. 'Coming, Mother.'

I mouth, 'Kaleen Joyce?' My eyes are squinting.

But Kaleen shakes her head like I did to her at Old Ma Izzy's. 'She's been calling me that lately. Adding my middle name. I think she wishes she gave me a double one like she did Coral Lee.'

While Kaleen is gone, I wander over to her bookcase – it's lined with Agatha Christies and Conan Doyles. But along with top contemporaries like Lee Child and Ruth Rendell, she's supporting the Australian crime writers too – there are Peter Temples and Kerry Greenwoods. I'm musing, thinking about seeing some Kaleen Pingellys on the shelves soon as well, when Kaleen flings open the door.

'That was Old Ma Izzy on the phone. The Cremello – I mean, Spirit – has escaped. He was heading our way.'

'How long ago?' I say, hastily placing back a Leigh Redhead.

'A few minutes or so, just before she called. She'd put him out in the riding yard and he seemed relaxed, eating some hay, and then he cantered around once and jumped the fence. Cleared it first go.'

'Hang on, Kaleen. Was that the same riding yard near the house? Those rails must be over two metres high.'

'Yeah, I know,' Kaleen says, her face pink. 'Perhaps we should have called him Pegasus instead.'

I run over to the French doors and look out. The Category Two is digging up a stump using a long-handled crowbar and a shovel. Mrs Pingelly is nowhere in sight. I stare down the winding driveway. I hear hoof beats and see a horse coming towards us, tail a flame of white, like propulsion. He gallops straight up to Watson's stable, and brings his hinds directly beneath him in a controlled sliding halt.

Watson manages to look ecstatic, as far as any horse can. His ears are forward, neck extended. The two horses touch noses, like a kiss. Watson squeals in a good imitation of a mare in season. I can hear the wooden door of his stable being battered, as he knocks it with a front hoof. Spirit just snorts, leans over the door and begins to scratch Watson's withers with his teeth. A few seconds later, Watson returns the favour.

'Are you sure Watson's a gelding, Kaleen?' I say.

She giggles and pushes my shoulder in a soft punch.

Old Ma Izzy skims her truck into the driveway and climbs out. She glances towards the house then strolls over to the stable yard. I see she has a halter and lead rope slung over one arm.

Kaleen and I run out to meet her.

'Hello, Spirit. You have wings on your feet. And Watson, how are you being today, my fine young gentleman?' She looks over the stable door down at his hoofs. 'Yours not so fleet.'

I'm wondering how she knows. And she doesn't seem to have any trouble remembering the horses' names. I guess it all depends on priorities.

'Ah, Karla and Velvet. You got back safely then.' It's not a question.

I feel mildly uncomfortable that she's remembered my name and not Kaleen's.

As we approach Spirit, he turns round, takes a few steps towards me and stops. I blink. It appears he's glowing, but that can't be right. My ability of seeing auras only extends to people.

We both stand, he and I. Facing. He comes over to my outstretched hand and then nuzzles my shoulder. It feels almost as friendly as when Kaleen soft-punched me a minute ago. My breath has caught in my throat and everything seems like it has ceased, like you see in movies when time is frozen. I can see Kaleen and Old Ma Izzy to the side of my vision. I know they're staring at me.

Old Ma Izzy is nodding. She steps forward. 'Here,' she says to me, cracking the stillness like ice, 'take this halter.'

I hold it up and Spirit slips his nose into it. Then everything moves in camera-shuttered scenes.

Kaleen takes the lead rope from me and walks Spirit over to the covered riding arena. 'He can't get out from here,' she says.

Spirit hangs back. Looks over his shoulder as if to make sure I'm following.

Old Ma Izzy says her goodbyes to the horses.

The alarm on my watch tings. It's six o'clock. I have to go home.

**6**

While I'm cycling home, my mind is whirring with the wheels. I can still feel Spirit's blue eyes meeting mine, see the faint glow like phosphorescence on his body, recall his coat beneath my hand, soft as clouds as I stroked him goodbye. He'll probably be gone by the time I get to Kaleen's tomorrow. Such a horse would be so valuable.

As I'm coming in the back door, Dad and Danny are going out through the front. I can hear them arguing. Probably about footy. They both barrack for opposite teams. Unfortunately, both teams have made the finals this year. I'm guessing they're heading for the hotel to watch the match on the big screen and slam beers on the bar whenever the other team scores. Danny has been going there with Dad a lot lately, since his age made it okay for him to drink.

Mum's working shift, which is usual for Monday evening. This means she and Dad would have had a hot meal at lunchtime. Mine will be in the fridge ready to heat up. Danny, who works at the local garage, would have already eaten his. He's always hungry.

I finish my dinner and look around our lounge room, think how Kaleen's house is so different to mine. God, her whole life is different to mine. She's talented, smart, good at sports – well, basketball and riding – and she has Watson, or any of the other eight stock horses to ride. This makes me wonder why she chose Ganymede for me. Could it be she really wants to get back at Donovan? I shake my head. I can't work her out lately. Last week she was saying how she was glad it wasn't Jim the gardener having an affair with her mother, and that she thought Donovan was hot.

I take my plate to the sink and get out my dessert. See the mountain of dishes ready for me to wash. My turn tonight. My turn every night, seeing

Danny is working these holidays. I close my eyes briefly and visualise Kaleen's kitchen, her huge dishwasher. Oh, to never have to wash dishes again, bliss!

Lying back in Dad's favourite armchair, I start to daydream about having Spirit as my very own horse, but I stop myself. It's never going to happen. I should be thankful I have Kaleen and her horses; at least I can go riding.

My iPhone buzzes. It nearly falls off the coffee table as I scrabble to retrieve it. It's a text from Kaleen: 'I'm asking Father if he'll buy Spirit for me. Early birthday present. Come over tomorrow at ten.'

I slump back into the chair. Bloody hell. My envy is screaming in letters as big as the house. Why, why does Kaleen get all the breaks? An early birthday present is right. Her birthday's in November and it's only the end of January.

I go over to the TV cabinet and open the glass doors, trying not to smear them. My job to dust and polish since I'm on holidays and old enough to help out, as Mum keeps reminding me. I shuffle the DVDs, come up with my favourite. A 1944 movie called *National Velvet*. Kaleen likes the movie too, although she does prefer the book by Enid Bagnold, which she says is utterly the best writing she's ever read. The heroine is Velvet Brown, same name as mine. She wins this horse – The Pie, she calls him – in a raffle and trains him to win the Grand National steeplechase in England. You know, naming me after a girl like that, you'd think they'd buy me a horse.

I think of Kaleen again and despair descends like a black cloak. Then I feel all kinds of awful. Kaleen's lost her book, her father is a Category One, the worst kind, Up Your Own Arse monster (although Kaleen doesn't know it) and her mother seems uninterested. Well, in Kaleen anyway. But then, are my parents any better? I mean, where are they now? Dad has Danny, and his other drinking mates. Mum has her job. She's always going on about how she loves working at the hospital. And she catches up with all her friends for croquet every Sunday.

It's a long movie and towards the end I fall asleep and only wake after it's finished. I glance at my watch, think of texting Kaleen back, but then I remember I haven't got any credit and my pocket money isn't due till Friday. I decide to head to bed, make tomorrow come quicker. Later, as I drift to sleep, my mind rears pictures of Kaleen winning at the local shows, astride Spirit, doing clear rounds and the fastest times.

I arrive at Kaleen's place at five to ten. I see Ganymede is in the stable next to Watson's. 'What are you doing here, old boy?' I say, rubbing his slightly dished nose. Such a strange blaze.

Kaleen pops up in Watson's stable, scaring me nearly witless.

'Shit, Kaleen, can't you knock or something?'

'What?' she says, looking gormless. 'You know, Vel, it's amazing how different everyone sounds when you only focus on your hearing.'

I try and make sense of this, but Kaleen continues, 'You know, you make a shuffle noise, really quiet. It must be those cheap jeans of yours.'

I've just about had enough of Kaleen, but I manage to keep my voice neutral. 'Yeah, no doubt. Anyway, do you want to find out what's happening with your would-be publisher? I have my laptop here if you want to take a look at your emails.' I lift the aforementioned article from my backpack. 'I would have texted you before to say I was bringing it over but, as you know, I've run out of credit.'

Kaleen looks a little contrite, but not sad. In fact, she has a faint yellow halo. The classic aura of happiness.

'Oh, my God, Kaleen,' I say, 'you've already asked your dad about Spirit. And he's said yes, hasn't he?' My heart sinks and rises at the same time. At least one of us would own him.

Kaleen bounds out of the stable. Watson tries to follow, but she expertly closes him in and gives him a sugar-free mint through the opening. 'Yes, yes, yes!' Her voice is high pitched like a plover's. 'The Quarter horse guy is coming over on Saturday to negotiate with Father.' She hugs herself and does a little dance on the spot. 'And you know what's funny too, Vel? Old Ma Izzy came over early this morning with that Western saddle we saw on her fence and that strange bridle. It's called a Bosal. She said we'd be needing it now. How did she know? And then she showed me how to put it on and how to use it.'

'Bosal?'

'Yeah, it's a proper one too, about fifty years old. Rawhide plaited nose band and, according to Old Ma Izzy, perfectly balanced.'

'Gee, that's almost antique. How did Spirit go with it?'

'Like an absolute dream. But then Donovan got on him and showed me what Spirit can really do. Spin on the spot, sliding stops. All that Western stuff. He said he wouldn't be surprised if Spirit had been a cutting horse. You know, those horses that work the cattle like sheepdogs work sheep.'

I'm standing there with my mouth half open. I'm so surprised she let Donovan anywhere near Spirit.

Kaleen goes quiet for a second and looks up at the sky. Her smile matches her colour. Then she looks serious. 'And there's something else, too, Vel. Something I've learned about Donovan.'

'What about Donovan?'

'Well, this morning I was cleaning out Watson's feet. I was about to straighten up when I heard that scratchy raspy sound of Donovan's riding chaps. He'd come up to check Ganny. So I kept down. I could see him through the cracks in the stable wall.'

'Yeah, how come Ganny is locked up?'

'Well, that's what I was wondering too. I'd already checked out Ganny's feet. He's got no signs of laminitis. And Donovan had the stable door top shut too.'

'Poor Ganny.'

'You don't know the half of it. I'm watching though this crack and Donovan puts Ganny's halter on him and ties him to the tether ring. Then he takes out a small pot of something gooey, puts on a rubber glove, dips his fingers in it and goes around to Ganny's hindquarters. Well, I'd seen enough.'

'What did you do?'

'I yelled out, "What the bleary heck are you doing?" Or something like that. That's when Ganny jumped sideways, nearly onto Donovan, and poor Watson almost ran up the back of his stall.'

'Hell, Kaleen, what happened then?'

'The strangest thing. Donovan came into Watson's stable and I nearly crapped myself. Didn't know what was happening. I was ready to scream out again when he put his hand over my mouth. And then he told me his story. You know, before he came here. How he was working on a stud farm.'

'You don't mean where Spirit came from?'

'No, Vel, in Western Australia somewhere. Anyway, he hated the way they treated their horses. Especially Ganymede, not his real name. So he stole him and did a runner.'

'Bloody hell, Kaleen. Well, he's a bit of a hero then. That explains Ganymede's name and why he's so touchy.'

'It also explains why Donovan didn't want us to ride him in case we suspected anything. Like he wasn't a stock horse. Or if anyone saw him when we were out.'

'So what was Donovan doing with the goo?'

'It was hair dye. He wanted to blot out Ganny's blaze mark in case anyone came around looking. He knew this Quarter horse guy, Mr Marika, would be coming to get Spirit, so he didn't want to take any chances.'

'Bit of a long shot that Mr Marika would recognise him.'

'Well, no, not really. Donovan's former place bred Arabs as well as Quarter horses. Ganymede's sire is Tareek Hazzan, a well known imported Arabian stallion. He's got the same blaze as Ganny's. His progeny are known for it. And remember Old Ma Izzy said that Mr Marika breeds Arabs too, not only Quarter horses.'

'So what was Donovan doing at Ganny's back end, anyway? Seems a bit suss.'

'Going to dye his socks first.'

For a moment, I'm speechless but thankfully I remember in time that she's referring to Ganymede's white markings just above his hoofs.

I glance down at his hinds. No sign of socks now, just black brown legs down to the ground. 'So how come Donovan hasn't done his blaze yet?'

'I told him that Mr Marika isn't due until Saturday. Also he ran out of dye. He used up all the colour he had on the socks. More than he thought. He's off now getting another batch. And some for me too.' Kaleen touches her bleached lock of hair, winding it around her fingers.

I put back the laptop. We start to walk towards where I can hear Spirit whinnying softly. It seems as if he's calling me. My envy is threatening to turn into jealousy. They call that the green-eyed monster. Never seen one of those.

Kaleen puts her hand on my shoulder, but I shrug it off. I don't feel chummy. I'm still smarting over her earlier comment about my jeans.

Then, rubbing salt into the welts of my envy, she says nonchalantly, 'Speaking of breeding, Vel, Spirit has top bloodlines too. Another imported stallion, Doc watchamacallit, can't remember it offhand.'

Wow, for a moment I wonder if Kaleen's father will even be able to afford Spirit. Then I look around Kaleen's humungous property, the stables, the seemingly never-ending fields of many thousand acres. The covered riding arena. That building alone would have cost a quarter of a million.

Spirit comes to me and nuzzles my arm, almost snuggling into the crook of it. I scratch his poll, the part between his ears. He stretches out his neck. I feel Kaleen's eyes on me.

'He really does like you, doesn't he?' There's a wistful sound to her voice and I feel somewhat vindicated.

She brings over the Bosal and I slip it on. It's easier than a conventional bridle to put on, as it has no bit. It has a big knot under the chin and, joined to that, long thick rope reins. The Western saddle is not that much different to our stock ones; this one has buckles and back surcingle.

Kaleen lets me have the first ride, as she's already had a turn this morning.

Spirit is unlike any horse I've ever ridden. He glides along; even his trot is easy to sit, his canter is rocking-horse smooth without the dips and he pulls up with my voice alone, or a slight shift of my weight in the saddle. It's like I've been driving Volkswagen Beetles (not that I'm old enough to drive yet, but you know what I mean) and now I have a Ferrari, but there's no sense of danger. In short, Spirit makes me feel like I'm a much better rider than I am.

Kaleen is sitting on the fence. As I canter past, she calls out, 'Looking good!' But her voice sounds different, like she's weighing something up in her mind and it's heavier than she first thought.

The next week skims past in a white blur of riding, intercepted by seeing the Category Two, Angry at the Drop of a Rat, would-be gardener becoming increasingly redder every day. Mrs Pingelly has given him two weeks' trial. For the most, he seems to be keeping it together. He's not a young guy and he's probably been moderated by years and mishaps. Losing your temper always hurts yourself in the end. Just like jealousy. I'm feeling the pricks of my envy increasing to huge gashes of self-sympathy along with my yearning. The only commiseration I have is that Spirit definitely goes better for me, more than even Donovan, who knows what he's doing. I seem to be able to think what I want Spirit to do, like go from a walk to a canter, and he does it. I can see it's driving Kaleen mad. And I'm not sorry. But then I question my loyalty and that's driving me crazy. There are moments (although lightning brief) when I wish Spirit had never come into our lives.

# 7

It's Friday today. Mr Marika, the Quarter horse bloke, will be here tomorrow. Even though Donovan has dyed Ganny's face he's still taken him off some distance away, to the Pingellys' other property. Talk about being cautious. But I guess if I'd stolen a horse I'd feel the same. Just for the briefest of seconds, I imagine doing that with Spirit. But the notion is as foolish as it is impractical. A horse is a hard thing to hide.

Watson's feet have come good and Kaleen has been riding him again. We've been swapping horses and seeing who can do best. Like jumping the light wooden poles we've set up in the arena, without knocking them down, or walking across the bridge in Mrs Pingelly's garden without shying at the four-metre-wide ornamental creek flowing below. That sort of stuff. Spirit always wins, even when Kaleen is riding him.

The gardener has finished the mowing; he's glaring at us and glowing like a stop light, even though we've been careful not to go on the lawn.

I dare Kaleen to jump the creek and Watson does it easily, with legs flying. He's a great horse really. For the first time today, I see Kaleen smile. She stops Watson, sits back, takes out her iPhone and starts to video us.

Spirit is looking towards the creek, ears forward. He feels ready beneath me, light, but bunched. Kinetic energy.

In my peripheral vision I can see the gardener to the right of us. He's having another go at the tree stump, using the long-handled crowbar which is nearly as tall as himself, and has his back to us. Even from many metres away it seems to me like he's on fire, his aura's so red. He's swearing too, but nothing I haven't heard before from the mouths of Dad and Danny.

I set Spirit into a canter and lean slightly forward, making sure not to pull on the reins. I don't have to check him; he's collected enough to make the jump without taking off too soon, or too late.

About ten metres from the creek, the gardener suddenly lets out a huge roar and, without looking, hurls the crowbar backwards behind him, like a javelin. It's coming straight towards us. With the cold realisation of the moment, I see that we have no time to avoid it.

Splitting a second, Spirit's right ear flickers, his head lowers, he seems to be making adjustments in his mind. Then he leaps. I'm almost left behind, it's such a huge arc, but I manage to grab the pommel in time. The crowbar passes low beneath us, like a massive steel arrow. I've never jumped a horse this high before. We land and now the creek appears right in front of us. I can hear my heartbeat in my ears and my vision is blurry. But Spirit clears the creek as easily as a skip.

Kaleen yells out from behind me, 'Oh, my gosh, holy heck, Vel, that was amazing! I've got it all on video.' She holds up her iPhone. 'This is going straight onto YouTube.'

I can't answer. I slump over Spirit's neck and bury my face into his thick white mane.

When I raise my head, I see the would-be gardener looking at where the crowbar has landed. I don't think Kaleen will have to worry about him becoming a working fixture. It's landed crossways on Mrs Pingelly's favourite daphne bush, the one just beginning to bud. Even I know how hard it is to get those things to flower. I have to stifle a laugh. But it's an ironic one. The bloody idiot hasn't even realised how close he came to spearing us like a kebab. But then, that's what a Category Two is famous for. No self-control and very little remorse.


The next day, I stay home, avoiding the clock and doing my chores. The polishing and dusting seem to help time fly, even though I have to damp mop the skirting boards as well. Mum's pretty fussy when someone else is doing the cleaning.

Kaleen has told me to be at her place late afternoon.

As I work, I muse up a thought: what if the Quarter horse guy doesn't want to sell? But then I recall Mr Pingelly's limitless chequebook and I squash that notion along with a particularly evil-looking black spider that has crawled out fast from beneath the TV stand where I've been waving the duster.

As I scrape up the body, my iPhone buzzes, making me jump. Another text from Kaleen: 'Police brought back laptop & memory sticks 2day everything in order ttyl'.

By three o'clock, I can't find anything more to do. I've even cleaned under the cookie tin on top of the fridge. My impatience has grown with every tick of our grandfather clock which sits, newly shining, in a dust-free lounge room.

I text Kaleen that I'm coming (I have twenty dollars credit now, yay!) and then, without waiting for her reply, I head out. On the way to my bike, I give a bleatingly hopeful Sebby a very early dinner. He rewards me with his strange little goat's noise, like a cat's purr.

Kaleen meets me halfway down her driveway. She's riding Watson and leading Spirit. 'Here you go,' she says, handing me the lead rope. It must be my turn.

Her face says more than any words and I know, with certainty like day, that she has got her early birthday present. But I'm happy for her, I really am. And most of all I'm happy for Spirit too. He'll have a wonderful home.

I prop my bike up against the fence and swing aboard. Kaleen hands me a large white envelope.

'What's this?' I ask, thinking Mr Pingelly must have given her a birthday card as well. That was taking it a bit too far. His guilt must be as huge as the sky.

I breathe in deeply and inwardly nod as I'm opening the envelope. I pull out several papers joined with a staple. There are two drawn outlines of a horse and official-looking writing. Names and dates. It's Spirit's registration papers, Scanning through, I whistle at his pedigree. And wonder at his price. I also see his registration name and smile. It's a clever combination of his sire and dam's names.

Kaleen is grinning like ten Ronald McDonald clowns, and I'm sure she would be jumping up and down on the spot, if she wasn't saddle-bound. I can't blame her, Spirit is one in a trillion.

'Well,' she says. 'What do you think?'

I hold the registration papers out to her. 'I think you are the luckiest girl alive, and Spirit's pretty lucky too.' I'm so pleased that I mean it. Integrity intact.

Then Kaleen laughs. 'Oh, you blurry goose, you don't get it, do you?' She pushes the papers back to me. 'He's yours, Vel. I'm giving him to you, as your early birthday present.'

I stare at Kaleen, words choking my throat. 'But he's yours, Kaleen,' I finally rasp out. 'And I can't have a horse. Dad won't let me.' At the same time, I'm crying big little-girl tears that are splashing onto Spirit's neck.

'Don't worry about that. I've got it all worked out. Spirit will stay here at my place.'

I open my mouth, but Kaleen shuts it with her next words. 'My parents will think he's mine, your parents will think he's mine, but he'll be yours. I'm giving him to you. Just think of it as the biggest re-gift in history.'

'But...but you...love Spirit. You really wanted him. I don't understand.' Meanwhile, my heart is pounding, beating the mantra, stop questioning, stop questioning, stop questioning!

Kaleen's voice is quiet. 'I've seen how he's been going this week, how you two have bonded. I'd never have that with him. And anyway, me and Watson are a team. I can't replace him.' Kaleen takes a piece of carrot from her pocket and leans down. Watson turns his head and gently lips it from her hand. 'And yesterday, Vel, the way he saved you both. There's something between you. He's yours in spirit as well as in name.'

'Hell, Kaleen, that's pretty lame.'

'Yeah,' Kaleen says, screwing up her nose, 'I don't think I'll be using that line in any of my stories.'

'Okay to use it in mine, though. My life one.' And I mean that too.

I slump down on Spirit's neck, feel his soft white mane once again soaking up my tears. Oh, my god, I have a horse! And not just any horse, the most beautiful, wondrous, gorgeous horse in the world with the most amazing eyes. And I have the best, best friend in the world too! I'm grinning now, my heart is beating happy beats through my tears and then I lean over and give Kaleen such a gigantic hug that I nearly pull her from Watson's back.

**8**

It's the second day back at school. These holidays have gone way too fast, but they've been ace, though. The best ever, now that I have my own horse. I'm writing this while I'm waiting for the school bus to arrive, then I'll put my notes into the time capsule Kaleen bought on eBay for me. It's a plastic box in the shape of a rocket. Flat bottom and pointed top. There's a hinged flap at the back, cleverly camouflaged with drawings of leaves and straight lines. It's from the early eighties when these things were popular; they took it pretty seriously apparently. Mum said, at her school when she was about nine, they buried one as big as a rubbish bin, with their letters in it to kids of the future. Trouble is, the school closed down ten years ago and the time capsule was forgotten. And she tells me now she can't remember what she wrote, or where it's buried.

I'll have to make sure that doesn't happen to my capsule. This one's about the size of a large Coke bottle and unfortunately it doesn't have a key. I'm not really worried about anyone discovering it. Mum never comes in here and I clean my room myself on Saturday mornings and change my own sheets. Also Danny would never snoop around. Too frightened of catching Girl Germs. His words. Despite being eighteen, he's pretty young really.

While I've been getting ready for school, I've been listening to Lady Gaga. (For the kids of the future reading this, she's a famous singer, rather brill, actually, and a really nice person as well.) She calls all her followers Little Monsters. She doesn't know how close to the truth this is in some cases.

I have a theory that true monsters are born, not made. I know some people can morph into them, like Coral Lee, who's a Category Three, Away in the Clouds monster, but like in her case it's often only temporary and usually modified. Although if it sets in, like it has with Mr Pingelly, the Category One, I'm not sure if it sticks long term. I'll have to get back to you on that. But I believe real, dyed-in-the-nastiness or annoyingness monsters, are born like that. Monsterish. And will never change. Thankfully, true monsters are not common. At our school, I've counted about one in every forty kids, so around ten all together, and only one teacher, Mr Hanker Wanker.

I have seen a baby monster – well, a baby who was a monster, to be exact. He was repulsive. I mean, even more so than most newborns are. I remember drawing back a breath when the mother lifted the blanket to show my mum, her friend, her new arrival. They were saying how cute and adorable the baby was, but all I could see were lines and mixed colours. Like a badly shaped blancmange. He looked like a Category Four, Head in the Sand monster. I mean they don't look as bad as Category One, but I was so shocked to see it at all, I spun around and ran off. Mum's friend said something to Mum about me being such a rude young girl, and Mum was cross with me for hours after. I'm not sure how the kid turned out, as they moved six months later, but I've never forgotten it. Oh, here comes the school bus. Have to go…

The bus is on time, which is unusual. Spider Johnson must be off sick or something and Mr Tangelo the bus driver hasn't had to stop umpteen dozen times and tell him off.

Mr Tangelo took over the bus run two weeks before the holidays. That first morning he stood in the aisle fronting us, arms folded, mono-brow rising and falling in time with his words: 'Listen up. No more bloody nonsense from you bloody kids, or I bring bloody bus to stopping.'

So far, he's stuck to it. His wife, Mrs Tangelo, who was our previous bus driver, had a nervous breakdown or something. Whatever that is. But she'd looked extra weird and extra twitchy before her husband took over, so it can't be anything good.

I sit in my usual seat, about the middle. The bus has a hierarchy. The most popular kids sit at the back. There they slide along the bench, cursing and giggling and sending spit bombs and other, more lethal projectiles, or pointed insults, onto the less popular kids in front of them. It pays to keep your head down. Try not to be noticed.

Donovan is giving Kaleen a lift into school today as he has things to do in town, so I'm on my own this morning. I hunch down and get out my maths book. I have to catch up on homework. That's the one good thing about getting the bus to school: it gives you time to do stuff like that. The ride takes three-quarters of an hour on a good day, like today without Spider Johnson, or up to two hours with him, especially since Mr Tangelo took over and won't be taking 'no bloody nonsense'.

I'm dying to tell someone about Spirit. That's the only trouble with this arrangement. I can't share how I'm feeling with anyone. And also I've wondered what if Kaleen and I split up as friends? Who would believe me? I might even be accused of stealing Spirit's papers. I shrug away the thought. Kaleen would never do anything like that. Even if she is acting a bit strange lately, she's always been a loyal friend.

As I walk through the school gates, I try and shrink into myself when I see who's up ahead of me. How they got there before me, when I was first to leave the bus, is a mystery, although I have been dragging my feet. There, on the stairs, leading to the main foyer, is Clarissa 'Kiss' Rothchile, surrounded by her girlfriends, like satellites around the earth.

She looks straight at me and holds up her iPhone. 'Hi, Velveteen.' Her top lip curls as she drawls out the words. 'Seen you on YouTube,' she says, wiggling her phone. 'Great horse. Pity about the rider.'

Her four acolytes snigger like performing pets and hold up their iPhones, facing them towards me as well. Even from this distance, I can see my beautiful Spirit, stretching in unbelievable style, multiplied by four, over what looks like mid-air. You can't see the steel projectile flinging beneath us.

Cheryl, Clarissa's main follower, screeches, 'Gee, Kiss, good thing Velveteen had that pommel to hang on to.'

The others burst out laughing, toss their bags over their shoulders and turn to walk up the stairs into their first lesson.

I'm so pleased they aren't in the same class as me. I'm in year 9AB. They're all in year 9GF. Even Clarissa's dad (I've heard he's more well off than the Pingellys) couldn't get her put up higher. GF's the lowest. Some things money can't buy. Like brains.

I feel a bit mean thinking this, but pull myself out of it when I hear Kiss's voice around the corner, out of sight but not hearing, saying to Cheryl, 'Let's post something on there,' in the sort of voice which promises poison.

But she had said Spirit was a great horse. If only Kiss knew. If only I could tell her he's mine.

# 9

As Kaleen's given me an early birthday present, of unlimited magnitude on the top friend scale, I've bought her an early birthday present as well. There's a play coming up in October (which still qualifies as early, seeing Kaleen's birthday is in November) at the Adelaide Festival Theatre. One of Agatha Christie's most famous. *The Mousetrap*. It's being advertised as a diamond sixtieth anniversary presentation. Sounds awesome. Kaleen will love it. I've got the money for the tickets and the bus fares for her and myself. Savings from my horse fund, money I've been putting away for three years to buy a horse. I was planning on having enough to get one by the time I reached twenty, had a job and could pay for stabling myself. But now I won't be needing the money.

I can see Kaleen through the window of our classroom. She's bent over her desk and writing like mad.

At recess, we sit at our favourite place under the cedar trees which flank the oval, well away from the schoolyard. Kaleen plays with the wrapper on her vanilla square, peeling little corners off the edges and rolling them between her fingers. I hope she's not going on one of her crazy diets again. Like the one where she didn't eat anything for a week, except chilli paste and lettuce leaves.

I look at her mid-bite of my vanilla square. 'What's up with you?' I mumble as I catch a crumb of custard on my lip and hook it with my teeth into my mouth. 'Was it awful travelling in with Donovan? You should have got the bus – no Spider Johnson, and Kiss and Co. waited till it got here before biting.'

Kaleen puts a small ball of paper in line with the others she's placed on the bench, and looks up. 'What did they say, Vel? Are they still calling you Velveteen?'

'Yeah, but I don't mind. It's better than what they used to call me. I mean, I am Velvet and a teen.'

'Sheesh, and you reckon I'm lame.' Kaleen peels back the remaining paper on her vanilla square and begins to eat.

'They've found that footage of me and Spirit on YouTube. Wish you hadn't posted it.'

'Why not? It's had over five thousand hits already.'

I roll my eyes, finish the last of my vanilla square and wipe my hands on my paper towel. 'That would be Kiss and Co. checking it out all the time, and making fun of my riding.'

Kaleen almost chokes. 'Kiss can't talk. Even though her dad's got her a twenty-thousand-dollar horse, she still can't cut it. Looks like a sack of potatoes. Poor horse. Won't have any sort of mouth by the time she's finished with it. What happened to the other one? What was she called? Blue Dreamer?' I nod, and Kaleen continues. 'She ruined that mare so much I think she had to be destroyed. Vel, you did blurry brilliantly to stay on. Kiss would have fallen off just riding Spirit.'

I know Kaleen is exaggerating. Before the terrible accident which took the life of Holmes, Kaleen's first horse, she and Kiss were fierce rivals on the show scene. But while Holmes and Kaleen were naturally brilliant together, a real team, Kiss always bought her talent.

I shiver, screw up our empty wrappings and aim them at the bin. I miss. I'm not having much luck today. 'So, what was Donovan like this morning?'

'Oh, Donovan's all right. I think I was feeling jealous before, because he was getting all of Mother's attention. Now I'm wondering what he sees in her. Do you know, she's got him doing the gardening? He was happy to get away. Quite chatty on the way in.'

I wipe my mouth, hold up my face to Kaleen. She checks me out and nods. Looks at me in expectation.

'All clean,' I say, and she smiles. I'm pleased she's cheered up a bit.

'Being a groundsman is only temporary, until Mother gets a new gardener. Or gets the old one back.'

'But Jim's run off with Chocka, hasn't he?'

Kaleen's eyes brighten. 'That's one good thing that's happened, Vel. Donovan told me Mother's getting a private dick – you know, an investigator – onto it. See if he can track them down. See where they've run off to. And then she's going to offer Jim double wages and even a part-time job for Chocka too. That's if Father won't have him back at the factory.'

I shiver again and turn around so my look won't give away my feelings. For a flash of a second, I consider telling Kaleen everything. But what do I really know? It's all supposition based on her father being a Category One and something I read in the paper. About bikies being in league with high-flying business men. What I need is real proof. One thing I'm pretty sure, though: it's not safe for Chocka and Jim to come back to the Pingellys. Maybe they should stay missing.

Kaleen looks reflective. 'Wonder what the PI will be like? Maybe I can tag along with Mother when he delivers his findings.'

The bell buzzes and we head back to class. I zip in front of Kaleen, but too late to avoid Kiss, who shoulders past me like I don't exist.

'Hi, Kaleen. Saw your new horse on YouTube. Great jumper. Don't know why you're letting Velveteen Half-caste ride him.' Kiss spins a derisive glance in my direction then continues talking at Kaleen. 'He's not as good as Sylvania Star, my new mare, though. When are you going to try and win back the Perpetual?'

The Perpetual's an agricultural show trophy. A beautiful silver cup with names of each winner etched into its mahogany base. It's awarded annually to the top horse and rider of the local show circuit. The winner gets to keep it for a year. And then it's up for grabs again. There are rules and regulations I'm not really clear about. All I do know is that Kaleen had been in the running to win it back off Kiss when she lost Holmes.

Kaleen shrugs and keeps walking.

Kiss trots behind her like an annoying toddler. 'This new one of yours looks better than Watson. He was never much of a jumper.'

Kaleen spins around on her heels and Kiss almost runs into her.

Kaleen's eyes are shining like steel and her aura has turned as red as a Category Two's. 'Don't bring Watson into this, you selfish bitch. There are things way more important than bloody shows. And jumping, and your goddamn stupid self. And Velvet's a way better rider than you'll ever be.'

Kiss puffs up into Kaleen's face. Chest out. 'Don't take it out on me, Kaleen Pingelly. Just because you were too careless to look after a good horse when you had one.'

Kaleen's hands drop to her sides. Her face has drained colour. Her mouth is closed.

Kiss strides off without looking back and Cheryl joins her on the steps.

'Slags,' Cheryl spits out in our direction.

I put my arm around Kaleen's shoulders. I can feel her trembling through the cloth of her shirt. 'Come on, Kaleen, don't worry about her. She's not worth it. Hey, do you know you swore just then? Twice actually. If you count goddamn as a swear word.'

I'm not surprised about Kiss's outburst. She's one of the ten kids who are monsters. A Category Three, Away in the Clouds monster. Doesn't care what she says or how it hurts. Pretty good at finding what cuts to the core too.

If only I could explain to Kaleen what I see when I look at Kiss. What I see when I look at any monster. I mean with a Category One, like Mr Pingelly and Hanker Wanker, it's all jagged lines and purple colours. But it's not static; those lines are merging and shimmering like a mirage, although they clear up long enough for me to discern what category type. Their colours, unlike the auras I see around normal people, bleed into and out of themselves with shades of black and grey. That's about the closest I can get to explaining it. I guess it's like trying to tell a person who's been deaf all their lives what music sounds like. What sound sounds like. I know I've heard from boys, and that includes my own brother Danny, that Kiss is pretty fly. Gorgeous, in fact. But I don't see it. I've never seen it. Right from when we were in kindergarten together she's looked ugly to me. That's why I'm fairly sure Kiss was born that way.

Category Threes, like Kiss, are the most misty of all the monsters.

Their hue is like when you mix all the colours of plasticine together. Not rainbow, but a kind of dirty brown. Their features keep twisting. To me, Kiss's mouth is lipless, her chin dips and curves. I can't look at her for a more than a nanosecond, she's so distorted.

# 10

The rest of the week goes by in bumps and grinds. The grinds are maths and history tests, PE lessons and a visit by the school inspector, which makes the teachers, even the really nice ones, start acting like singers before a Queen's performance. The bumps are Kiss and Co. bad-mouthing me every time they see me, which although I make sure is minimal, is still enough to be damn annoying. She's dropped Velveteen and is back to calling me Half-caste.

My dad's maternal grandmother was Indigenous, Pitjantatjara, from north-western South Australia. So I'm not exactly half. And my green eyes belie my ancestors' beautiful brown ones. But there are those, like Kiss and Co., who know and love to judge. It's a small town not only in its dimensions. And it's any god's guess what they'd call me if they knew about my ability. Probably crazy insane. Who would believe it?

Also Kiss keeps tormenting Kaleen, bringing up about Holmes, saying how it was Kaleen's fault that he'd been killed, and deliberately calling him Sherlock in condescending tones. God, the lipless gap which is Kiss's mouth turns her cheeks inside out when she does this, and it takes all my willpower not to laugh in her face. There's irony in her nickname that those without my ability will never understand. And it's times like these I wish I could draw. I'd sketch up a picture for Kaleen, to show her how Kiss really looks to me. Well, as much as possible. That would cheer Kaleen up. She's been plaited into herself with grief since Tuesday and Kiss's first remarks about Holmes, and today, Friday, she didn't even come to school. I texted her, but she hasn't answered.

Saturday morning, I rush through my room cleaning and dump my sheets into the washing machine on top of the towels. I move Sebby to another patch of grass and take the knots out of his tether line. I refresh his water bucket, taking care to keep it at the end of his reach so he won't knock it over. I swear at my bike when I see the tyre's flat, but then I breathe in relief when it seems to be staying up after I've pumped it. I've got to get to Kaleen's. I'm really worried now. I've been awake half the night.

The wind pushes me along, helping me get to Kaleen's place in extra-fast time.

I pedal up to the French doors and knock on the glass. I can't see anyone and Kaleen's not in her office. There's an unfamiliar car out the front. But not the coppers; it doesn't have that look – too many dents and paint scraped off to be theirs. I know the government is cutting back on police funding but not to that degree.

I go around to the front door, prop my bike on its stand, and for a moment contemplate just walking in as Kaleen does at my place. But I can't do it. I'm not sure what Mrs Pingelly really thinks of me, but if I did that, it would definitely confirm it in the negative.

Through the glass I can see the dining room and Mrs Pingelly's back. There's a strange woman sitting, facing towards me. Kaleen is next to her and they are all drinking coffee and eating cake. Apple turnover, Mrs Pingelly's speciality. Kaleen looks up and moves her hand in a come-in gesture.

The woman turns out to be the private detective, by the name of J.D. Claridge. JD for short. Kaleen seems fine, smiling and talking, butting in really, until Mrs Pingelly asks Kaleen in her poshest tone why doesn't she take her friend (Has she forgotten my name? Surely not, I've been coming here since I was five) for a ride? Kaleen gets up slowly and we leave the table. I take my piece of cake with me.

Kaleen's mood slumps, along with her shoulders, back into gloom. It's not until we're on the horses that she straightens a little. 'Vel,' she says, her voice flat. 'We'll head out to Old Ma Izzy's. She rang me last night. She wants some help drenching her horses. She's got those new wormers with the Boticide in them. We need to get some for our horses soon, too.'

I go quiet. I hadn't thought of Spirit's ongoing costs. Maybe I do need to be careful with my money. I can't expect Kaleen to pay for everything.

As if reading my thoughts, Kaleen says, 'She's going to pay us. We can have a job there every second Saturday if we want.'

Without waiting for my answer, she pushes Watson into a canter and flies over the first of the log jumps that are alongside the forest path leading to Old Ma Izzy's place. On the way, there are a dozen or more of various girths and heights, and I have to keep my wits and balance about me. Mostly, Spirit clears them economically, but occasionally he seems to over-jump, leaving what almost feels like a horse size beneath us. I'm not sure if he's remembering the crowbar incident, or if he's just being super-careful. Watson's in fine form, clearing everything neatly; he appears to be energised and happy, in vibrant contrast to his rider.

When we're nearing Old Ma Izzy's, Kaleen slows Watson to a walk. Then she takes him over to the last log jump, slides from his back and slumps down onto it. Spirit's ears flicker and, without me prompting, he walks us over and rubs Kaleen's shoulder with his nose. I dismount and sit next to her. She's staring straight ahead, her eyes glazed, her face as pale as death. I gently push Spirit's nose aside and put my arm around her.

I know who she's thinking about. Holmes or Holmsey, as she called him, was the most wonderful of horses. A beautiful reddish bay, like his genes hadn't made up their mind for him to be chestnut, he still had the definite black points, mane and tail and long dark legs. A breathtaking presence. Without ever having to lay his ears back, Holmes was always top horse in any paddock. He was super-intelligent and cool, just like his namesake.

Kaleen speaks, her voice monochrome. 'I know it's been two years but, you know, Vel, I still hear Holmsey some nights. I'm sure it's him. He had this certain neigh. You remember.' She lifts her eyes to mine, I nod, and she continues, 'And he was so smart. When I first got him, I was only six, but even then I knew he was special. Much brighter than the stock horses. He worked out straight away how to get to the other field, through all those gates, where the hay shed was. Father was so angry because he had to change all the latches.' Kaleen's lips curl a little smile. 'And he never shied at anything. Remember that helicopter checking the power lines? Holmsey didn't blink an eyelid. He was always thinking. Sussing things out. He never wasted any energy. Not that he was lazy.' Kaleen grabs my wrist and half squeezes it in a kind of self-protest. 'He conserved his strength, knew his limits. And his limits were so high it didn't matter.'

I rub her hand. I don't know what to say. I've never seen Kaleen like this, so vulnerable. I can only guess what she's going through. And this is the first time, in the two years since the accident, that she's talked about Holmes. Thing is, she's never said exactly what happened that day. I only found out that Holmes had died when I came for a visit on Sunday, the day after. Mrs Pingelly told me Kaleen had gone off to her Auntie Margie's for a break. She also told me that Holmes had been killed. But she'd shut the door before I could ask how. I remember walking my bike home in shock. I did find out later Holmes had died in a horse trailer accident.

There have never been any horse trailers at the Pingellys' since then, and Kaleen's never gone to another show. Also, all her trophies, her ribbons and anything associated with Holmes seem to have disappeared. Even his saddle and bridle. I figure she must have sold them. She's never talked about Holmes since that terrible day until now. If I ever brought him up, she'd go quiet. I have some pics saved on my computer, but I've been careful to keep them out of sight. They're saved in a file I've named Conan Doyle. I reckon I'll know the time when I can show them to Kaleen. When she's ready.

Kaleen rubs a hand over her eyes, takes out a tissue and blows her nose. She swings aboard Watson and turns his head towards Old Ma Izzy's.

Spirit whinnies as we approach her place. Dogs start barking and there's a rerun of horses and deep-throated neighs from hidden stallions. Apparently there's more than one. It promises to be an interesting afternoon.

'Ah, girls,' Old Ma Izzy says from outside her doorway. 'I'm so glad you've arrived. Looks as though we won't be drenching today. Although,' and she laughs, 'we may be getting drenched ourselves if we stay out here. Old Thor, methinks, will roll up soon.'

'Thor, the god of thunder?' I start to protest. 'But there's been sunshine all the way.'

I glance skywards. Then I feel a cold gust like the sweep of a giant's cape. The trees whistle and a smack of wetness hits my forehead, quickly followed by another heavy drop. We manage to get the horses to a stable and make it inside the house, when rain cascades like a waterfall. It seems to be arguing with the wind, competing for the most noise, but then the thunder butts in and wins the debate. Thor has arrived.

I shiver and pull my jacket around me. Kaleen sits down on the nearest chair, a large old flock one, sprouting more dog hairs than its original coat.

A multicoloured cat slides down from the top of a kitchen dresser, stretches and comes to rub herself (tortoiseshell males are very rare) on Kaleen's legs. She leaves a faint airborne trail of fur as she languidly steps away towards her food. Near the entrance doorway on a silver plate, the size of a dinner one, lies a heap of meaty morsels, which she snaffles down in a most unfeline way. Although a portly tummy belies any hunger.

'Now, Archibald Thomas.' Old Ma Izzy sniffs. 'You'll be getting the colic like your poor mother.'

I amend my thoughts as I watch him walk away, tail held high in objection, the proof of his (now empty) maledom, in rounds of flat black fuzz, clear for all to see.

The rain batters the roof and it's hard to hear ourselves speak. Kaleen hasn't tried and I can see Old Ma Izzy looking at her. I'm guessing she's picked up on Kaleen's mood.

Old Ma Izzy lifts her voice. 'I would move from there, Karla, if I were you. Paladin approaches.'

What sounds like twenty hard-footed possums with swishing fur seems to be coming from somewhere alongside the house.

A door slams shut in a swing-like noise and a small pony gallops into the room, head down, towards the chair where Kaleen is sitting. He's the same hue as all the hair which appears to be growing on it. Two dogs of mixed huge breeds, but different colours to the pony, bring up the rear and stand momentarily panting and surveying Old Ma Izzy with quizzical brown eyes. They clear water from their noses in short sneezes and shake myriad drops of rain from their coats, showering us both.

Kaleen leaps sideways off the chair almost at the same time as the hairy pony slides into it. He perches, teetering, before folding his forelegs beneath him.

At closer quarters, I see Paladin is a Falabella. A miniature horse. Every bit of him exquisitely horse-like, but so tiny. The chair gives out a groan and slips back in a squeak. It's only protest.

Outside, the rain eases.

Old Ma Izzy lowers her voice and waves her hand in his direction as she turns to the sink. 'Karla and Velvet, meet Paladin.' She fills up the kettle and plugs it in. 'Would you girls like some herbal tea?' she asks, holding up a box with pictures of raspberries like cherry blossoms on it.

Kaleen and I nod. We scrape out some high-backed seats from the breakfast bar and sit down.

The kitchen area is super-clean. The sink gleams and there are no dirty dishes anywhere. Garlic is braided in long strands, like macramé, off the ends of the curtain rods, and dishes of fresh fruit roost on the dresser and the table, like advertisements for good health.

It's my turn to go quiet. I feel a bit miffed at being so wrong with my assumptions. Assuming the chair belonged to a dog, thinking the cat was female. And the blasted rain. I was sure the weather girl hadn't forecast a shower, let alone a storm. I peer at Old Ma Izzy with doubled respect.

She smiles. 'Now, Velvet, don't be worrying any. 'Tis normal to get things incorrect sometimes.'

How did she know? I hadn't said a word. Well, not about the hairy chair or the cat or the pony…horse.

I swallow hard. And smile back my pride. Take a sip of my tea. It's delicious.

Kaleen is still quiet, but some colour has filtered to her cheeks. I'd also heard her stifle a giggle as she scratched Paladin under his chin, before sitting down next to me. And now I can almost hear her thoughts: Old Ma Izzy does have horses inside.

I really wish I could have been the one to cheer her up. And here's another false assumption: I'd thought Old Ma Izzy had channelled into Kaleen's depression. But it seemed I was wrong on that count too.

Old Ma Izzy puts a massive pink-iced cake, topped with strawberries, in front of us, and with a gleaming knife slices huge pieces onto three plates. Even the plates have rosy flowers on them. Pink's the theme, it seems today, or maybe she likes it. Pink's okay, anyway. It's red that indicates danger and anger, or Category Twos. I think of Kiss, the Category Three, her dingy brown aura like dirty dishwater. I suppose she'll be at the Ginninderra show today on Sylvania Star, scratching up enough points to keep the Perpetual for another year. How is it that nasty people seem to get all the breaks?

Kaleen picks at her piece of cake. She appears to be chewing and not swallowing. I fill in for her, telling Old Ma Izzy how well Spirit is doing, and how Donovan's been such a wonderful help. Old Ma Izzy says little, but nods and eats. I notice she gives more cake to the dogs, who sit straight-backed on either side of her, than she eats herself.

The dogs' expressions are level with the table and have expectancy and contentment rolled into them. The sort of look which says life's good and it doesn't get much better than this. That's how I've been feeling since I got Spirit. But now I'm feeling guilty too, for being so happy when Kaleen's so miserable. I can't help it, and a little part of me is even resentful because Kaleen can't share my happiness. Mostly, though, I'm pissed off with Kiss, who has brought all of this on, or more correctly, up. I'm also wondering if Kaleen has ever really dealt with it. Not with Kiss, but Holmesy's death.

Old Ma Izzy takes my plate and hers to the sink. 'Ah, Velvet,' she says, zipping up the blind to its full height and letting some pallid sunshine sneak in. 'There's a bit of blue on the horizon there. Should give you time to check on Watson and Spirit. You can fill up their hay racks, if you want.'

Kaleen half rises to join me, but Old Ma Izzy places her hand on her shoulder and gently pushes her down. 'Tarry a while longer, Kaleen. You have to be finishing your cake. Velvet will see to Watson.'

I leave the house quickly, fully aware I've assumed again. But this time

I'm pleased I've got it wrong. Old Ma Izzy does know how rotten Kaleen is feeling. And she's even got Kaleen's name right.

When I get to the door, I glance back. Kaleen is talking as Old Ma Izzy lifts the hair from her face with her strong lean hands. Even from here, I can see Kaleen's tears glinting in the cuts of light streaming through the window.

It feels soft outside. The wind has dropped and the sky has cracked the clouds. I check the horses. Give both a rub down. Top up their hay racks and carry buckets of water to them filled from the barrel, which is overflowing from the stable's downpipe.

I walk round the outside of the house to use up more time. I've only been about a half an hour. Not long enough for grief. Out the front, I pass by the sitting room. On the bay windowsill, through the glass, I see photos of horses facing towards me, like a shop window display. I count over a dozen pictures, some with several horses in each frame. I look behind me at Old Ma Izzy's horses busily grazing in the paddock, their rugs glistening like seal skins. I can't recognise them as any of the horses in the photos. And why are the pictures facing outwards? That would mean you wouldn't see them from inside the house. Only the backs of the frames. And few visitors would venture around here.

I hear footsteps. A hand touches me, but I'm not surprised. I know it's Old Ma Izzy.

'There is a reason they're facing this way,' she says. 'Look, Velvet, behind you, the paddocks. The hills. What do you see?'

I turn round, stare, taking in the horses, the fields, the windbreaks of trees. Then I realise that from this perspective you can't see the fences. The rolling valleys seem to swallow them up. The expanse goes on forever and into the sky.

'Freedom,' I say quietly.

For a moment, Old Ma Izzy gazes into the horizon. There's more blue emerging, like a far off sea.

'And so they are,' she says, 'Free. My beloved horses. My departed ones. All that have gone before, all here. Even the naughty ones.' She pauses and I feel her pain like a slow deep ache in my stomach. Then she smiles. 'Especially the naughty ones. They're all with me.'

I see now why the photos are facing through the window. The horses are looking out, together across infinity, and there with the living.

'Kaleen needs some time alone, Velvet. Here, I'll tell you about these horses, the great and the small, but all their own horse, as we should all be our own person.'

In the middle of the windowsill, a black and white photo stands out in contrast to the coloured ones. The frame is ornate and gleams in wood polish and care. The lone horse, unremarkable in any way, except its stance, seems to be staring straight into our eyes. The person who took the photo must have been standing directly in front of it.

Old Ma Izzy touches the outside of the window closest to the frame. 'Everyone has their golden horse. Oh, I too would deny it, if pushed. Truly all have been special. They have. But I cannot deny my heart. My Freya has her own place there.'

'Freya was the name of a Norse goddess, wasn't it?'

'Yes, Velvet, still is, for those who believe.' Then almost as if she's reciting a poem, Old Ma Izzy continues, 'Freya, more beautiful than Troy's Helen. Fertility and love.' She turns around, points in the paddock to a small chestnut mare, grazing apart from the others. 'There's one of my Freya's descendants. Her great, great granddaughter.'

It's hard to see a likeness, so I turn back to the window. 'That's an old photo,' I say, stating the obvious. 'Black and white. When was it taken?'

'Ah, Velvet, long before you she's been gone. But I had her the twenty years. It was a goodly time. She was twelve when she found me.'

I lean on the glass, cupping my hands around my eyes. The sun is glaring now and, coupled with the faded picture, it's making it hard to see.

'She looks so sweet.'

Old Ma Izzy sighs. 'And she was that and all. And so much more than words. We knew each other fine. Like you with Spirit. The trust that comes from knowing and connecting. You never forget. As you never forget any of them. No matter how many may come your way.'

We stand in silence. In homage.

I think of Spirit. He is my first. Will there be others? I'm not ready for what that may mean.

Kaleen comes up, leading Watson and Spirit. They're both saddled. I bring my gaze back to the window, and Kaleen stands with us while time shifts and the horses gently blow their breaths of steam on the cold glass until we see no more than mist.

11

Later, Old Ma Izzy walks us to the gate. 'Off you go now, girls. While the sky is kind. There'll be time aplenty to return to your homes without getting damp.'

We put the horses into a working trot.

Kaleen is the first to speak. She definitely sounds better. 'I wonder if Old Ma Izzy has a doggy windowsill too?'

'I'm sure she has,' I say, smiling as Spirit successfully snatches a long piece of grass growing at the side of the track. The Bosal makes it a lot easier for him to eat on the run.

Halfway home, we slow to a walk. But it's a brisk one. The sun is still holding up, but the breeze has got the cold in it like ice, and blowing stronger by the minute, threatening to be wind.

'She's ace, Old Ma Izzy, you know. Way cool,' Kaleen says. 'It's like she knew exactly what to say. Made me feel heaps better. I can't believe I told her so easily.'

I think about the tears, but I don't mention them.

'And Vel, I want to tell you all about it now. I don't know why I couldn't before.'

Kaleen rides up alongside and our horses fall into step. With the strengthening breeze, it's necessary so we can hear each other. Spirit's ears are forward like he's not listening and Watson's are doing the same.

'Go on, Kaleen,' I say, and Spirit's ear flickers back, just for an instant, as if it were on a spring.

'As you know, Vel, it happened at the last one of the agricultural shows. Holmsey and I had to go, to get enough points to win the Perpetual. To beat Kiss, we only needed to place. By then, she was having problems with her horse, Blue Dreamer, and the last few times I'd beaten her easily. But I'd missed some events, so we were almost even.'

Kaleen pauses and I see her take a carrot from her pocket and give it to Watson. He lips it from her hand like it's his due. And when Spirit looks back at me in question, I do the same.

'I'd missed some of the shows because I'd been having trouble with our horse trailer. First, it got a flat tyre and I was too late for my events. And then the brakes were faulty and the garage was taking ages to fix them. So I'd missed the Gawella show and the Port Ellion one too. I couldn't miss the last one.'

I gasp. That must have been what happened – the brakes must have failed. Oh, my god, poor Holmesy.

Kaleen seems to pick up on my vibe. 'It's not what you think, Vel. I mean, it was a horse trailer accident, but not our horse trailer.'

When I finally speak, it comes out like a frog's croak. 'I don't understand, Kaleen. Not your trailer? Whose was it then?'

'One of the shearers'. He seldom used it. But I was so desperate I asked him if we could borrow it. He even offered to drive us. He had to really. Something to do with the tow bar coupling and the electrical system not being compatible with our four-wheel drive. His trailer was pretty old.'

Kaleen stops talking for many minutes. When she starts again, it's her voice now which sounds like it's disappearing. 'Oh god, Vel, if only I could go back. I've blamed myself for so long.'

Now I'm wondering if I even want to hear the rest. I have this memory of something I read in the paper several weeks ago. About a horse which had partly gone through the rusted floor of an old horse trailer. The owners had no idea until they stopped. And the worst thing was, the horse had managed to stay on his feet. The three that were left, that is. I swallow the bile which rises with the image. I grit my teeth, grasp my reins, not pulling on them. But Spirit feels my tension, lifts his head and gathers his stride. I drop my hands onto his neck and he relaxes.

'Go on, Kaleen,' I say, in a whisper.

Kaleen's words are steady like she's measuring them and wanting them to come up right. 'The trailer didn't break down. We had a car accident on the way to the show. A teenager on his L plates. No qualified driver in the car. He didn't give way. The shearer and I were okay. But the horse trailer was side-swiped. If only I hadn't wanted to win that stupid Perpetual.' Kaleen shakes her head. 'You know, I burned everything after it happened. All the photos, my trophies, ribbons. Even Holmesy's saddle and bridle. And I deleted all my show pics.' Kaleen hiccups like she has something stuck in her throat. 'I thought if I got rid of everything that reminded me of Holmesy it would stop the hurting.' Her voice breaks again. 'Now I wish I'd kept something.'

She turns away and pushes Watson into a trot and then a canter. Breaking all the rules of not rushing home. Spirit gently tugs on the reins, stretching out his nose. What the hell, I think. I let him have his head and nudge his sides. He needs little encouragement. And soon we're flying, beating the wind, the memories, and the tears and rain which fall scalding and frozen around our faces.


Sunday it's storming all day, and in the afternoon Mrs Pingelly drops Kaleen off at my place.

She looks okay. I've told Mum what's happened, how Kaleen had finally opened up about Holmesy's death. So, after bringing us some hot chocolate with marshmallows, Mum leaves us alone. She does love me.

As if channelling my thoughts, Kaleen says, 'You know, Vel, another thing I've learned from all of this is that Mother does care. Do you know, Old Ma Izzy told me Mother had contacted her about me? She'd told her I'd been feeling down. And wondered if she could help. And Mother's even remembered it's Holmes's eighth anniversary soon.'

I look up, eyes wide.

'Not when he died, you goose,' Kaleen says firmly. 'But when I got him.'

'Oh.' It's all I can manage.

'And Old Ma Izzy did help, Vel. Made me see it was just an accident. How I couldn't have known. How things happen sometimes and we don't know why. And how Holmsey's shade lives on.'

I think about this. Shade, shadow, soul.

'And I really believe her, Vel. Like I said, I hear him some nights. And in his stable I know he's there.' Kaleen begins to cry. Silent tears.

I get up and hug her. Feel her trembling, like she did when Kiss had first given her a hard time about Holmes.

She snuffles loudly, wipes her nose. 'It's okay, Vel. I should have done this years ago when it happened. It's long overdue. That's what Old Ma Izzy said. And she said it will get better. Lessen up. Until you remember only the good times.'

I recall some lines from an ancient cowboy song my Great Aunty June would sing, when I used to stay for holidays with my older cousins, before she passed away.

> There's a bridle hanging on the wall,
> and a saddle in a lonely stall…

But Poor Kaleen has nothing to remember Holmsey by. I suddenly know what I'm going to give Kaleen for an early birthday present. The tickets for the Agatha Christie play can wait till later in the year and be an early Christmas present instead.

It's Monday morning and it looks like it's going to take two hours to get to school. Spider Johnson's back, and he's in top form. Mr Tangelo's sticking to his 'I no move the bloody bus' promise, which has happened three times already, and explains why it's late picking me up.

Kaleen is like an over-extended balloon, her face pink and her hands waving as she beckons me to sit with her at the back of the bus. It's practically empty today.

'Guess what, guess what!' she says, grabbing my arm and pulling me down onto the seat. 'Kiss didn't win the Perpetual after all. Brandon Quinn won it.'

For a moment, my head spins. Brandon Quinn, he's in year 11AB, two years higher than us. Cool and hot at the same time. Top horseman. Beach blond, eyes green, square-jawed and such a nice guy too. Always helping out, raising money for good causes. Wish I could be one.

'Couldn't have happened to a nicer guy,' I say, my eyes swimming with pictures of love and lust.

Kaleen peers at me then relaxes, leans back in the seat like she's swooning. 'Mm...I know,' she murmurs, arms raised above her head. A second later she sits up, voice strained like she's trying to square up some emotion. 'Something happened to Kiss. She had a bad fall at the water jump. Broke her leg. And nearly drowned at the same time. No one wanted to pull her out, apparently.'

'Bloody hell, Kaleen, surely not. I mean...'

Kaleen interrupts, a smile twitching at the corner of her mouth. 'I'm not sure really. But they did take ages to drag her out. And there was CPR. You know, resuscitation.'

'I know what CPR is, Kaleen. I've done first aid too.'

Kaleen suppresses a giggle. 'I just made that up. About the CPR. But not about her breaking her leg. In two places. And she did get an awful dunking.'

'Poor Kiss,' I say, but my heart's not in the words. And I go quiet, remembering how I'd questioned why nasty people seem to get all the breaks. Then seeing the irony, I have to stop myself from laughing.

'Don't feel too sorry for her, Vel. She wanted to send Sylvania Star off to be destroyed, like she did Blue Dreamer. But Brandon offered to buy the mare.'

I fall into silence once more. Brandon comes from as wealthy a family as the Pingellys. Although he's made a lot of money himself as well, selling apps. He's a guy who's going places. Wish I could tag along too. But with my looks, I know it's never going to happen.

The week flies, but not the mornings. The bus trip seems to be getting longer and longer. On Thursday, we get to school almost at recess.

Today, Friday, Spider Johnson's away again. But this time he's been kicked off the bus indefinitely, or until they get another bus driver, whichever comes first. Tonight I'm not catching the bus home, though. I'm going to wait at the hospital until Mum's shift finishes, and get a lift home with her. But before then I'm buying something in town, which will complete the present I'm putting together for Kaleen.

I love going to Mum's work. She takes me through the wards and tells me about all the illnesses. She knows everything about everyone on her floor. Being a cleaner is like being a spy without any subterfuge. Kaleen's actually jealous of me going to the hospital and being able to share it with Mum with no restrictions.

Some of the stuff nearly makes me puke. But it's also strangely fascinating. Like how there's this death rattle that a terminally ill patient makes just before they pass away. Mum has heard this heaps of times as she swishes the mop around or refills the jugs of water. She's been working here for almost twenty years, so the chances are pretty high that she's the last to see them alive. Especially the really old patients who have outlived friends and family. Kaleen has instructed me to watch out for this and, if I do hear it, to try and remember it, and imitate it exactly when I see her. Research, she calls it, for her next book or even for her current one, *Bitter the Taste of Murder*. She reckons she could always poke it in somewhere. But she needs to know how it sounds so she can write it with, as she says, 'authenticity'.

That evening, when I get home, it doesn't take long to put Kaleen's present together. I've even bought some special paper which will make it look professional. I can't wait for the morning. I'm hoping this weekend will be fine. I don't trust the weather girl any more, even though Danny says she has nice boobs, although what mammaries have got to do with meteorology, I'll never know.

Saturday morning, I look outside my window – it appears fine so that's good enough for me. This time, I get my sheets washed early (I got told off last Saturday for leaving them in the machine), get them out on the line, give my room a good clean and fix up Sebby for the day. I swear at the seemingly endless knots in his tether, think this may be a good metaphor for Kaleen to use, and then I head out on my bike. Kaleen's present is safely tucked away in my backpack.

Kaleen's on her computer when I get there and she calls me in through the French doors. I sneak a glance around to find where her present will feature best. Almost straight away, I see a great place for it. Awesome. I slip the package out of my pack but Kaleen is turned away to the computer, intent on bringing something up on the screen. Coming closer, I see it's her Gmail account.

'Look at this, Vel,' she says, leaning slightly aside so I don't have to read the screen over her shoulder.

It's an email from the Canadian publisher. A standard, although on the upper side of positive, rejection.

I tuck the present in my backpack again. Perhaps it's not the time to give it to her. 'Damn it, I'm so sorry, Kaleen. After all the work you did.'

'Oh, I don't care,' Kaleen says, although her tone sounds flat. She brushes away some hair which has fallen across her eyes and flicks up another email. It looks professional. 'He did me a favour. I didn't like his domain address, something dodgy there. Anyway, this publisher's better and he lives in Australia. In Adelaide even.'

I scan the email. It seems okay. The publishing house is called Wanda-Willow Press. The site features YA novels and crime fiction. One of the authors sounds familiar.

'Look, here he is.' Kaleen clicks up a picture of a middle-aged man with a red beard and moustache. 'Tarrant Moselle. Chief editor and publisher. He got back to me straight away. He wanted much the same info as the Canadian guy, so I sent off what I'd already put together. First few chapters. The synopsis and blurb. Too easy.'

Kaleen sighs. I know she's trying to be brave. And I have this feeling something else is bothering her as well.

Perhaps my present will cheer her up. I swing my backpack around and open the zip. I lift out the package but when I turn, I see Kaleen is gone. Then I see her shoes under the chair facing the computer. She's in sleuth mode again.

She's back before I feel the need to look for her. She's carrying a folder with 'Private – Confidential' written on the front in vibrant red letters. It's her clues folder, the one she writes things down in. Things she thinks may come in useful for her writing. I know there's a heading in there called Death Rattle.

She slips into her shoes and I follow her, feeling like her shadow, up to her bedroom where the folder usually lives. She keeps it under her bed away from the prying eyes of Coral Lee, and so that she can easily pull it out mid-dream or muse and jot down ideas. It has a pen attached to it with a silver chain.

Without looking at me, Kaleen falls back on her bed. I drop my backpack on the floor, gently place her present on top, and join her. Her folder is open on her chest and we both stare up at the ceiling.

She's the first to talk. 'Vel, you know I never liked Jim very much and I never really got to know Chocka. So I don't know why I'm so upset.'

I half sit, and prop myself up on my arm. 'What are you talking about, Kaleen? Did JD, that private investigator woman, find where Jim and Chocka ran off to? Is that what you mean? I bet Donovan will be pleased. No more garden duties.' My mind sketches up an oasis of palms and cocktails. And Jim and Chocka tanned to a crisp in oversized sombreros, toasting each other before slipping off towels and diving into a gleaming blue pool. But I quickly realise I've got no idea where gay guys go to escape.

Kaleen doesn't answer straight away. She closes the folder and then reopens it. Skims through a few pages. 'Yes, JD did find them.' Her voice sounds strange. 'I wrote it down this morning after Mother told me.'

I take the folder and it falls open to lots of black writing with hysterical swirls.

'Homicide is investigating it now,' Kaleen says quietly.

I flick over. At the top of her last entry I read the words 'Suspicious Circumstances', underlined a half a dozen times in thick black ink. The rest of the page is empty.

And then with a realisation as cold as night but as sure as frost, I know that Jim and Chocka are no longer missing. And no longer alive.

# 13

I haven't written for a while. Thought I'd better catch up with what's been happening. I've pasted my printed pages in this notebook, since Kaleen told me I should keep them together so they don't get lost. It's more like a proper journal now. And still fits in the time capsule if I bend it in half.

Kaleen's filled me in on JD Claridge's findings. JD discovered some clues when she checked out Jim's cottage. Packed suitcases under a blanket on top of the wardrobe and brochures on Hawaii, sort of making my daydream of where gay guys go for holidays, right, in a way. Well, it would have been had they got there. As it was, they didn't get much further than the Pingellys' property. I read somewhere that murderers like to do their killing close to where they live, something about not wanting to travel too far. I guess it makes sense with petrol prices the way they are. Although, if the killer is who I think it is, he never worries about the cost of anything.

Anyway, when JD checked all the local travel agents and couldn't find any bookings, she got suspicious and informed the police. They didn't take it seriously but, before she could find Jim and Chocka, someone walking their dog did. Shallow graves in the forest (the same one we ride through on our way to Old Ma Izzy's), like whoever did it wasn't too fussed how long it took before the bodies were discovered. Just think, we were riding past them for weeks. We've been working for Old Ma Izzy, helping out with the drenching – she has seventeen horses, and recently 'started' Zeus, a young colt. She doesn't use the term 'breaking in'.

Today is a student-free day, so I'm definitely giving Kaleen her present. Two weeks hasn't made much difference; it's still an early birthday one. I'm busting to give it to her, to see her reaction. And thank goodness it's decided to be summer (even though it's now autumn) and we can get some serious riding done…

I get to Kaleen's and she's out the front of her house with Watson and Spirit already saddled and waiting. But no more stalling; this present seems like it's burning a hole in my backpack. I bring out the package and thrust it into her hand.

Kaleen looks at it like it's a foreign object or something, although I would have thought the birthday wrap of horses, candles, and cakes would be a giveaway. It was expensive paper.

'Take it inside, Kaleen. I'll go and tether the horses. Don't open it until I get there.'

When I go in, I find Kaleen on her computer, the gift on her lap. She swirls around and holds it up. 'I get it, Vel, this is my early birthday present. Right.' There's a slight intonation in her voice like she's asking a question.

I nod and she rips off the paper with no intention of recycling it for rewrapping.

'Oh, Vel, it's wonderful. Thank you so much!' She gazes at me, her eyes filling. Then, with slow words: 'I remember when you took this. It was about three years ago.' She holds up the photo in its wooden frame.

I'd chosen this pic because it was such a natural pose, for both Kaleen and Holmesy. We'd been on a long ride that day and after we let the horses loose, Holmsey had rolled. Then, when he'd gone for a gallop, doing a lap of the paddock, I'd brought out my camera.

In the photo he has dry grass and leaves in his forelock and mane and his gorgeous coat is ruffled with damp and dirt. Kaleen's still wearing her riding helmet and has her arm around Holmsey's neck. She's chewing on a streak of hay and Holmsey, in sort of solidarity, has hay hanging from his mouth. But his head is held high and, like the picture of Old Ma Izzy's Freya, he is looking straight into the camera. In the distant background, in soft focus, is a very young Watson. He hadn't been broken in then – I mean 'started'.

I watch Kaleen take the photo around her office. She stops near one of the windows which look out over the stables and Watson's and Spirit's field. I hold my breath. Exactly where I'd thought it would be best. She places it down and stands back.

'Aren't you going to face it outwards, Kaleen? You know, turn it round so he can see the paddocks?'

Kaleen shakes her head, continues staring. When she does speak it's in quiet words. 'No, Vel. Maybe later. I need to have Holmsey with me for a while.' She's stroking the glass on the frame and smiling now.

'I'll pop out and check on the horses,' I say.

I go and stand with them, enjoying the warm sunshine and drinking in the day. A cool breeze shuffles up some leaves, sends them whispering and eddying to lap in sharp edged drifts of gold and brown around my feet. Donovan is working Cody in the stock horses' paddock and he waves to me in a sort of salute as he canters past. Watson and Spirit follow his every movement, looking like synchronised swimmers without the water.

Tiny pardalotes are having baths in the troughs, sending quicksilver sparks from their flickering wings. And currawongs are warbling and cocking their heads, watching me watching them. Red gum trees stretch back the past, an indeterminable age. My beautiful Australia.

I close my eyes, light turns twilight. I feel my ancestors, hear the thrumming of feet in beat with every living thing. And all around me the haunt of didgeridoos, the white straight flash of body paint. The angular bend of arms and legs, paying homage to the animals they hunted and the land in which they lived. I am joined by blood. The Dreaming.

Sometime later, Kaleen calls to me though the window. 'Hey, Vel, come and check this out.' She sounds excited. She's back on the computer and looking almost as intently at the screen as she had at Holmsey's picture. She grabs me and pulls me close. 'He's got back to me. You know, Tarrant Moselle, the publisher from Wanda-Willow Press. And he wants to read the rest of my novel. Isn't that great?'

I try to look enthusiastic, but the truth is I have a weird feeling about this guy. For a start, his name doesn't sound believable. I wish I could see if he's a monster or not. If only my ability extended to photos and pictures. But it doesn't. I need the flesh to get the vibes, I think.

As it is, I don't have to answer. Kaleen springs out of her chair like it's on fire, and dashes to the window. At the same time I hear hoof beats. I hope the horses haven't got loose.

'Old Ma Izzy's here. I forgot to tell you, but she rang last night and asked if we'd like to go for a ride with her. That's why I had the horses saddled and ready. We better take it easy on her. Remember she's an old lady.'

Kaleen dashes outside leaving me to shut the French doors. I glance back at Holmsey. It's uncanny how it looks like he's looking at me. 'Bye, Holmsey. Back soon,' I whisper. Tears burn my throat, but I swallow them down and go outdoors. Kaleen's nowhere in sight.

Old Ma Izzy is on her chestnut mare, the great, great granddaughter of Freya, also of the same name. One of her dogs, called Odin, is loping alongside. She's riding bareback. Freya's wearing an English bridle and there's a gold rope around her neck. I'm quite surprised about this. I wouldn't have thought Old Ma Izzy would need a neck rope to hang onto. I soon see the rope is not for holding onto, it's a means of control. The bridle is bitless and the reins are loose and short, but not tight, merely lying on Freya's neck, untouched.

Old Ma Izzy's quiet hands caress the golden cord like a newborn, her fingers extending and squeezing almost imperceptible signals. 'The reins and bridle are only for back-up safety, like the helmet,' she says. 'One never knows what encounters one may befall, when riding away from home.' She briefly touches her hard hat and then the golden cord. 'Now, Velvet, you are not to be trying the neck rope. Not yet. Many a year to train a horse to this.'

I nod, try and look serious. I'm beginning to wonder if Old Ma Izzy is quite sane. I squash this thought. She's eccentric, a whole different thing to being batty. And her aura is clear and clean, of the most brilliant hue, unlike any I've ever seen. There's not even a whiff of monster about it.

Kaleen emerges from Jim's cottage, muttering to herself, 'Oh, I know where I saw it last,' and then disappears into the stockmen's quarters. Soon she comes out carrying an old hat. 'I don't know why it was in Donovan's room,' she says.

I instantly recognise it as the oversized floppy one Jim always wore when gardening.

Old Ma Izzy dismounts and takes the hat from Kaleen. 'Are you sure it was his?' she asks, as she holds it in front of Odin.

Odin sits and sniffs, his neck extended and nose upturned as if he's been offered a leaf of spinach to eat, or something equally disagreeable to dogs.

We both nod and Old Ma Izzy says some words, indiscernible to us, to Odin who sniffs around in circles and lines, then bolts off like he's been stung with a cattle prod.

'I'm surprised he's picked it up so quickly,' Old Ma Izzy murmurs. 'But look sharply, girls! The hunt is on!'

Like a jockey, she swings onto Freya's bare back and the pair dash off after Odin, before we even have time to put a foot in the stirrup.

Soon we're all tearing along the path in the forest. Odin has his nose down like a bloodhound, but like a bloodhound he also has the unnerving habit of stopping dead. Our horses do the same, but Freya merely dances around the dog and is off again as soon as Odin's regained the scent.

At one of these stops, Kaleen whispers to me, 'What's Old Ma Izzy doing? They've already found Jim and Chocka's bodies. It's a bit off, making it into sport, isn't it?'

I've no time to answer before we're plunging headlong again, this time off the track and through the scrub. A box thorn bush as big as a picnic table appears round a corner. Odin flies over it and Old Ma Izzy and Freya do the same. It's like she's glued to the mare's back. I have no time to think before Spirit clears it like a kite and we're off once more, twisting and turning through high ferns and scrub. My heart is leaping in my chest, I can hardly count the beats, it's galloping so fast. My breath is ragged, but I'm also feeling more alive than ever. I'm hoping I stay that way.

Spirit is easily keeping up but I can hear Watson behind me, his breathing laboured.

'Hang on, Vel, we have to stop.' Kaleen's voice catches my ear.

I sit down, squeeze the reins and Spirit slides to a halt. Watson shoots past us and Kaleen turns him around and stops. She's red in the face and breathing almost as hard as her horse.

'Geez, Kaleen.' I stifle a giggle. 'I think we should have warned Old Ma Izzy to take it easy on us!'

'Fricken heck, yes. Poor old Watson.' She puffs. 'He's not very fit. All that time off in his stable.'

I fix my helmet, which has half fallen over my eyes. 'Oh, the run will do him good. Anyway, we better catch up. God knows where Old Ma Izzy and Odin are now.'

Then whistling through the trees we hear her words like an incantation.

'Halloo there. Spirit, Watson, come forth. Straight on now, there's good fellows.'

We enter a clearing that's surrounded by pine trees. The earth is disturbed, in a long rough rectangle, close to where Old Ma Izzy and Freya are standing. Tied around some bushes, a disjointed police tape is waving in the breeze like faded bunting at a gala.

Old Ma Izzy removes her riding hat and looks down at the grave. We ride over, dismount, and do the same. Now I know why she's brought us here. To pay our last respects. Two men have died. Brutally murdered. Murder is always brutal.

Unexpectedly, I'm smacked in my mind about my own mortality. I've talked to these men. We even ate together.

I sneak a peek at Kaleen. Now her face has turned white and her head is lowered.

Old Ma Izzy touches a finger to her mouth and we stand in silence, like we did those weeks ago back at her place in front of her horse window.

## 14

When Old Ma Izzy had been invited to dinner at the Pingellys' not long after Jim and Chocka were discovered, or should I say uncovered, Mrs Pingelly told her again that she was worried about Kaleen, this time in coping with the murders. She knew how much Old Ma Izzy had helped Kaleen come to terms with Holmsey's death, so I guess she was hoping she'd come up with something to help Kaleen deal with this too. I figure Kaleen's mother can't help Kaleen herself, so she does it in the only way she knows. By surrogate.

But quite frankly, even though I understand about the importance of closure (as my mum's self-help books would say), I'm getting tired of all this death stuff. All this dark and dagger. I'm wishing we could get back to normal, whatever that was. I'm also in fear of seeing Mr Pingelly every time I go to Kaleen's, although I know mostly he doesn't get home until late. And Kaleen's been moping around, which is understandable. I'm so relieved she seems happy about the photo, though, and not sad. It was one of the reasons I decided not to give her the present for a while after we'd heard about the murders. I didn't want to bring her down even more.

Now I want to focus on the positive, I'm going to shed my suspicions until after I've seen this new publisher, Tarrant Moselle, for myself. Kaleen's sending off the rest of her manuscript of *Bitter the Taste of Murder*, as soon as we get back. And if he accepts the novel, I'm sure there will be a Meet and Greet to sign contracts and stuff.

As we ride closer to Kaleen's place, I see Mr Pingelly's car slide up the driveway and slink into the garage. I get a glimpse of his latest Mercedes and his green vintage Jaguar as the door glides down behind him. I can't face his face today, or what passes for his face, amidst all the jagged purple of a Category One.

'Hey, Kaleen,' I say, keeping my tone light. 'I've gotta get home early today. Have to go to the supermarket with Mum.' It's only a white lie. If I do go now, I'll have to help with the shopping. But that's okay because I've thought of some things to buy which will definitely cheer us both up.

The shopping takes ages, Mum's one of those people who pick something up, hover it above the trolley and then put it back on the shelf. Then, a row down, she'll wheel around, go back and toss it in again. It's really infuriating.

I take the shopping list and burn off through the aisles, throwing in all the generic brands. Mum trails behind, picking the items out one by one, reading the labels and muttering something about foreign countries and hygiene. When I look in the trolley, she's put most of them back.

I give up, hand her the list and take a supermarket basket to the chocolate and sweet section. Lots of it is fifty per cent off. Wicked! Kaleen and I both like chocolate, but I know she loves the salty stuff, so I grab several packets of crisps too, although not the plain chicken or salt ones, she likes multi-flavoured, like chilli and lime. Marshmallows are on special as well, so I take a huge bag and throw it in with all the other stuff. It makes a pleasingly squishy sound as it lands on top.

Mum eyes my basket like a pilgrim might view a leper. She screeches her trolley to a stop. It doesn't take much. A twisted front wheel acting like a brake is happy to oblige.

'I've got no money for rubbish like that, Velvet Brown. Put it all back.' And when I don't move she says, 'Now!' in a voice which suffers no argument.

But I am ready for this and hold up my bag. 'I've got cash, Mum.'

It's amazing, the transformation. She relaxes and swirls the trolley forward. 'Yes, well I hope so,' she says. 'That's okay then.' She looks more closely into the basket and her eyes light up like sparklers on New Year's Eve. 'Mm, that chocolate looks nice, Vel.'

Poor Mum, I think. There's not much money for treats. Especially with Dad still out of work and the sheep not due for shearing until later in the year.

I take down an extra large bar of Nut Milk, her favourite. And I know she's mine. I can do almost anything. Which is just as well, with what I've got planned.

I text Kaleen and rush off to the checkout, narrowly beating Mum to it.

Kaleen texts back when I'm in the car and Mum's still loading shopping bags into the boot. I'll probably get told off for not helping, but I need to answer Kaleen before Mum asks any questions. I'm terrible at lying.

I chuckle when I read what Kaleen has written: 'thts gr8 no probs will B there'.

I text back 'Operation Midnight, G2g!' as Mum slips into the driver's seat.

Before she can ask, I hand her the Nut Milk chocolate and flash her my most innocent smile.

She says thanks then glances sideways at me, eyes narrowed. 'What are you grimacing for, Velvet? I hope you and that Kaleen Pingelly girl are not getting up to something.'

I go to bed at the usual time. I decide to read, but just in case I fall asleep I set the alarm on my watch for twenty to twelve. Under my bed I have the shopping bag with all the goodies. I've also made up a large bottle of lime cordial. I almost added some of Dad's vodka, but decided not to. Seeing him and Danny every Friday night staggering around, slurring their words and ending up blubbering like babies, is enough to put anyone off drinking. And then the next day trying to blame each other for the hangovers they have. Typical of Category Fours, even if Dad and Danny are very mild ones.

It seems as if only a few minutes have passed when my alarm starts to ping. I quickly turn it off and reset it to go off in twenty minutes' time. I hold my breath, listen for sounds. I'm hoping no one else has woken up. Then I hear a tap on my window.

Soon Kaleen and I are running across the field, scattering the sheep who have probably been counting themselves, because they're still awake. Finally we stop at Dad's bonfire heap. It's on the other side of the hay shed, well out of sight of the house.

Kaleen has brought her little beach tent. It's a two-man (or two-girl and some of their stuff) one, which fits into her school backpack with room to spare. It's super-light and easy to set up. You only have to unfold it and it springs open on its own, and it's ready to use. There's a pocket around the bottom of the tent, on the outside, to weigh it down (you fill that up with sand or rocks) so the wind won't blow it away. And it even has a front flap and a plastic over-cover for wet weather. Although Kaleen hasn't brought those tonight.

I get out the firelighters and the kindling I collected earlier. Soon the stack of broken branches, dry bark and dead bushes is flaming into the sky. We watch the sparks shoot into spirals sending out splintered gold and red like fireworks. It's a still night so they go straight upwards.

'Isn't there a fire ban still on?' Kaleen says, her voice suddenly as breathless as the air.

'Oh, shit and bollocks,' I yell and two sheep, who have followed us, scoot away from the fire like woolly white comets.

It had been such an unusually wet summer I'd totally forgotten about the fire bans. Even though the fire's warm, I feel cold all over. In a frenzy of feet, I kick dirt onto the heap and Kaleen does the same. Soon smoke is billowing and then, just as quickly, it dwindles to nothing. We slump down onto the fold-up chairs, which came with Kaleen's tent, look at each other and start to laugh. Our faces are black and tears from the smoke have cleaned little trails down our cheeks. There's soot in our hair and clothes and our shoes are covered in dirt and twigs.

I lean down to the shopping bag, pull out some paper towels and my heavy-duty torch. Simultaneously, my alarm goes off again. We jump, half topple off our chairs, grab each other and start to giggle. Then we roll in a tangle over the ground like little kids. It's midnight. The witching hour, and time for our feast!


Two hours later and stuffed like Christmas chickens, we lie back in the tent, with the flap open. The stars are visible pins of light in the inky blackness and we make the usual mutterings of never-ending and infinity, coupling our insignificance to it all. It's been a great evening so far, I think, and then I remember the marshmallows. Damn, I'd had images of us toasting them over the fire.

I rummage in the bag and skewer two marshmallows onto forks.

Kaleen groans and does her little theatrical act. Arms and eyes raised heavenwards. 'Oh, Vel, no. No more food!'

'Come on, Kaleen. Just one little marshmallow. And these are flavoured too. What do you want, the caramel or the strawberry?'

Kaleen props up on one elbow then slumps back again. 'How do you propose to toast them? No fire, remember.'

Like a conjuring act, I draw out the box of matches I'd used earlier.

Five matches later, I hand her a marshmallow. It's gross. Tastes like sulphur.

But I can't give up. 'I have candles,' I say triumphantly.

Half a bag of marshmallows on and we can hardly move. But we haven't had so much fun in ages. In fact, things going wrong are the glaze which has made the night shine even more.

'Wouldn't it be great if we could camp like this, away from home?' Kaleen says, and sighs.

I toss most of the rest of the marshmallows to the sheep, keeping some aside to give to Sebby. I inhale a deep cooling breath of the surrounding pine-scented air, nod and then realising Kaleen can't see me, switch on my torch. 'Oh yeah,' I say, my tone rising. 'It'd be rad. Just you and me.'

Kaleen sits up, holds her stomach and stifles a groan, but her voice is energised like the Kaleen of old. 'Oh, Vel, we could, you know. We really could! We could go on one of those quest thingies.'

'I think you're suffering from a sugar high,' I say, giggling. My cheeks hurt from so much laughter, but it's a pleasant ache.

I shine the torch into Kaleen's face, and I stop giggling. She's not laughing. I sit upright and try to pull my expression to serious. 'Bloody hell, Kaleen. You can't really mean it. What would the quest be for? How would we get there? And most importantly, what about the parentals?'

'Sheez, Vel, I haven't thought about all those things yet. Although I do know what the quest might be for.'

As if picking up on some mental picture, mental being the operative word, I instantly know what Kaleen is talking about. 'Oh, Kaleen. You're not thinking of visiting that publisher in the city on your own, are you?'

'No, of course not.' Kaleen looks down at the tent's floor. 'You'd be there,' she says, grinning.

She looks a little macabre in the torchlight and I shudder.

'What is it, Vel? Have you seen a monster in him, or something?' Then she answers herself. 'No, that's not possible. You can't tell through photos, can you?'

I almost feel like lying, but I can't. Anyway, her novel hasn't even been accepted yet, although I have a strong feeling it will be.

# 15

Kaleen hasn't been on the bus for the last few days and she's been really secretive at school, spending most of her time on her laptop with Google Earth. She's also been madly scribbling in her clues folder. If I try to take a peek, she puts her hand over what she's been writing, or closes the book like I'm trying to cheat off her or something.

Donovan's been giving her a lift in every morning, even though he doesn't need to get anything in town. It's like he's become her father now. Also, every time I ask to come over to her place after school, she has some excuse why I can't.

At lunchtime I can't stand it any more. It's worse than when she was working on her novel. At least then, in between writing bouts, she shared what she'd written with me.

We both finish our sandwiches at the same time. I take our wrappings to the bin and glance over at Kaleen. She's still smiling in a Mona Lisa sort of way, casting looks skywards from time to time and then scribbling madly away in her folder.

'Come on, Kaleen. Let me see.' I stand in front of her and try and grab her notes, but she's too quick, flings them away, and I fall forward, almost onto her lap.

Two boys pass by and I'm mortified to see one of them is Brandon. God, he rocks. The guy with him, a wiry dude, whistles, but I bet it's for Kaleen. She's been glowing lately. I'm pleased she's happy, but all this secrecy is getting ridiculous.

Kaleen sits up straight, her gaze following the guys' backs. They're heading over to the bike shed. They must have the afternoon off. She murmurs something which sounds like 'dreamy' and then looks me in the eye. 'Okay, Vel. I'm ready. Ask me anything.'

She opens her folder towards the back and I see sketches of maps and numbered paragraphs, like a writing assignment. There are columns of figures with totals, and what looks like a shopping list.

'Quest?' I draw out the one word.

Kaleen folds her hands. 'You were right, Vel. I want to meet up with the publisher in Adelaide. And before you ask, yes, he, Tarrant Moselle, the chief editor and publisher at Wanda-Willow Press, has accepted my book.'

I don't know whether to feel overjoyed or terrified. But Kaleen's face is lit up like the sun and I can't help myself, I instantly feel happy for her. I fling my arms around her and we hug tightly just as the two guys come past again, pushing impressive matt black racing bikes. I read the name, Scott, written in white letters along the frames. I've learned enough about bikes from Danny, who's an avid fan of the Tour de France, to know that's a top brand. Along with being a super horseman, Brandon also races bikes. There's no end to his awesomeness.

'Looks like Willem Van Den Hoven's riding bikes too now. Brandon must have talked him into it.' Kaleen's referring to the wiry dude.

Willem Van Den Hoven. I'd forgotten his name. He's only been here a month, an exchange student from Holland, staying at Brandon's place.

I watch them wheeling away. 'From what I know, Kaleen, cycling's pretty big in Holland. They even have bike ferries and two-storey buildings for parking bikes, like we do for our cars.'

Then I smile to myself. I remember Kaleen and I had watched a TV documentary on Holland, or the Netherlands as it's also called, a few years ago. And she knows heaps more than me about bikes. She's even been to France and seen the Tour, as she calls it, actually live.

Kaleen's stalling for time. Maybe she hasn't worked out this quest thing as well as she'd like me to believe.

'Okay,' I say slowly, bringing her back on track. 'So, how are we getting to Adelaide? The city bus?' I think of the bus tickets I've ordered for the Agatha Christie play in October. Perhaps I could use those, change them to an earlier date. Buy more bus tickets later for October, when I've earned extra money from Old Ma Izzy.

Kaleen rolls her eyes. Her voice drops to sarcasm. It's not a good sound, but it brings home her point. 'Yeah, sure we will. We'll hop on the bus and we'll be there in two hours, cosy and warm and safe. That's not a blurry quest, Vel. Quests are supposed to be difficult and hard. They're supposed to be challenging.'

'Mm…like the *Lord of the Rings*? Maybe we should get a donkey like Frodo did.'

Kaleen grabs me by the shoulders. 'Now you're getting closer.' She stops. Blinks twice. Her tone goes dubious. 'Frodo never had a donkey.'

I stare at her face, pull away and glide down onto the bench like a ballerina collapsing on stage. 'Oh no, Kaleen, you're not meaning to ride the horses there? It's nearly a two-hundred-kilometre round trip to Adelaide. All those busy highways. It would take days. Where would we sleep? What would we eat?'

'They used to do it in our great grandparents' day.' Kaleen sniffs and sits down next to me.

'Yeah, but they didn't have the lorries and road trains, Kaleen. And most of the roads were dirt. I don't feel like skidding everywhere on horseback. Horseshoes and tarmac don't mix.'

'I've thought of that, Vel.' Kaleen flicks back several pages in her clues folder. Stapled in the middle part there's a shining brochure about Pleasy Horse Boots.

Pleasy Boots turn out to be rubberised boots which fit over your horse's hoof and do up with clips. They have non-slip soles. The ad on the brochure shows a grinning cartoon horse wearing a Pleasy Boot, with his forefoot extended as if he was admiring it. Underneath were these words like a caption.

Pleasy Boots will please you and your horse. Pleasy Boots reduce the incidence of hoof concussion and slipping on the hardest of sealed roads. Pleasy Boots! Easy and Pleasy to boot!

Now, that was lame, but they'd stop the horses from going that way. And they did look pretty cool. Because it's sandy in the paddocks and in the forest, where we ride, we don't shoe our horses. They go barefoot most of the time. But if we were going to ride all the way to Adelaide, well. I pull up my thoughts. What the hell am I thinking?

The bell goes and Kaleen looks victorious as she collects her clues folder and heads back into our next class. Australian history. It's about some explorers on an expedition to find a way across the Outback. I avoid looking at Kaleen, although from the corner of my eye I can see she's trying to catch my attention, head nodding and smiling like a crazy person. I know she'll go on about synchronicity and this lesson being a sign about us going ahead with our quest, so I'm somewhat mollified, but not happy, when we find out these explorers never made it back. I could argue against the quest now and say this was a bad omen.

Much as I try, Kaleen won't talk about it on the way home in the bus. 'Too many big ears flapping,' she whispers. 'We have to keep this a secret.'

My stop is before hers, so I make a final plea while I'm getting off. My iPhone buzzes an answer as I'm walking up my driveway: 'Come ova afta dinna'. I'm not sure if this means she'll be coming here, or if she wants me to go there. Then I remember posh people eat really late. The Pingellys' dinner party, where I'd first met Chocka and Donovan, hadn't started till eight o'clock. Kaleen must want me to go to her place after my dinner. We have dinner – or, as Mum calls it, tea – at six.

My mind draws a line back to that night at Kaleen's. How I'd wondered at Chocka's name. He said he was from Croatia, but his last name definitely sounded Italian. And he'd told us his family was into security. I swallow heavily as I recall how I'd thought he might have been a bad guy. It seems I was dead wrong about that.

As it turns out, I can't go to Kaleen's. Dad found out about the bonfire heap today and is off his tree. As a Category Four, he hates confrontation, but he had no trouble fronting me with this. He's grounded me until Sunday, which means I'll even miss out working for Old Ma Izzy. The thing is, I'm not really upset. Actually, I'm surprised he took so long to find out. I deserve to be grounded. It was a bloody stupid thing I did. Bushfires are terrible, worse than anything you can imagine, and even though we live in a low fire-risk area, we've had some awful ones here. The last fire happened fifteen years before I was born, but every year since there's been a memorial for the ten people who died.

I am frustrated, though. It's like some greater hand is stalling for time, building the suspense. I guess that's how they do it in crime novels. But I'm busting to know what Kaleen's come up with.

# 16

Sunday, we're out early, riding the horses. Kaleen tells me she's been working them every day. Exercising them in the evening for at least two hours before dinner, leading Spirit off Watson. Spirit feels super fit and Watson's not puffing any more. Kaleen seems up to form too.

We head out to the main road. There's a strip of verge down each side, which Australian stockmen used to call the Long Paddock. In times of drought, they'd go droving, pushing their cattle along it for miles, living off the grass which had been growing there for years.

It's been newly slashed, but we still have to watch out for potholes and hidden wire from where the fences have been moved. Rubbish is not a problem like it is in our neighbouring states. We have litter fines in South Australia. Still, it pays to be careful. Yobs still throw out an occasional empty bottle and their hubcaps often come off.

'See, Vel,' Kaleen says, scanning ahead with her hand. 'Look at all this feed, chopped and ready to go.'

'Have to be careful of the poisoned stuff,' I say, countering.

'Oh, geez, Vel, not here. This is sweet enough for us to eat.' Kaleen laughs and slides off in an untidy heap onto the grass. She picks up a dry shoot and chews on it.

It reminds me of the photo of her and Holmsey. I'm pleased I don't feel that tightness in my stomach like I did before. The memories are coming good already, like old Ma Izzy said they would.

Watson leans down, sniffs Kaleen and then begins to nibble the grass. He doesn't seem hungry. I dismount and Spirit scoops up a large mouthful, lowers his head and begins to munch.

A semi-trailer powers past, engine roaring and its white canvas cover flapping like a giant demented goose. Both horses look up for a moment, gaze at its departure and then resume grazing.

Kaleen waves her hand again, this time at them and I know what she's saying without the words. They are wonderfully quiet.

I catch hold of her hand. 'Okay, Kaleen, talk. Everything. No stalling. And I'm not asking any questions. You're giving me the answers.'

'Right then, Vel. Sit, and listen.'

I undo Spirit's lead rope, which is tied to his halter and looped around his neck, and I do the same for Watson. Kaleen watches me. She's lying back, hands behind her head and peering skywards.

I let the horses out to their ropes' length, with me as the tethering pin.

'Quest,' she says, her voice even. 'To get to the publisher and sign the deal for my novel. Mode of transport: horses. Supplies carried by packhorse. Cody will be perfect.'

I begin to speak. I want to say how young Cody is, but she holds up her hand.

'Let me finish. Donovan's been doing lots with Cody, he's heaps quieter now. He's been working him at the local sale yards. I can also ask to borrow Donovan's saddlebags. Feed, we have plenty along the way, thanks to the wet summer. We have my tent for shelter. And we can put up overnight at the sale yards in Adelaide when we get there. I've lined it up with Donovan.'

This time I do butt in. 'You've told Donovan? Are you crazy?' It's then I realise I'll be going on the quest. I slump back on the grass in defeat.

'No, of course not,' Kaleen says, 'Only teasing.' She smiles. 'But I know a way in. The last time I was at the auction with Father, I saw this hole in the fence, down at the back of the sheep pens. Easy to make it bigger with a pair of wire cutters. No one's going to notice a few horses. And we can hide the tent in the trees. There's water there as well.'

'How long?'

Kaleen sits up. 'How long before we go? Or how long to get to Adelaide?'

'Both,' I say, with a sigh.

'Well, I reckon the horses will be fit enough in another couple of weeks. So any time after that. Round trip two days. And it's exactly ninety-two kilometres there, which means, if we go at a slow to medium trot, say between twelve to fourteen kilometres an hour, it will take around seven hours. Of course we'll have to have feed and rest breaks. And I thought we could get off and lead the horses sometimes, too, especially up the hills. So add another three hours.' Kaleen is speaking easily without having to calculate. She certainly has it all worked out.

I nod and wave her on.

'So, Vel,' Kaleen puts on a professional voice, 'the morning after we get there, and as early as possible, we tee it up with Tarrant to meet us at a hotel or café. You, as my agent, will check him out. If all things are unmonsterish, we'll sign the necessaries and head back. It's bound to be quicker going home.'

'The parentals?' I ask weakly, my voice a squeak.

'What about them?' For a moment, Kaleen looks lost. 'Oh, they're the least of our problems. We do the old "you're staying at my place and I'm staying at yours". Then we make sure we call them up a few times so they don't ring our landlines. And we'll say what a great time we're having, riding. We won't even be lying.'

When we arrive back at Kaleen's, she gets on her computer and prints me up pages of quest stuff. I'm actually looking forward to it now. I mean, my New Year's resolution was to do more with my ability, help Kaleen out, so it seems right somehow. Although I still have reservations.

'Read this when you get back to your place,' Kaleen says, slapping some sheets of paper into my hands. 'We'll talk about it tomorrow, at school.'

When I get home, I mutter something about homework to Mum. She nods and keeps on peeling the vegies. I should help, but I can't wait, I want to know all the finer details right now.

The first sheet is titled What We Need To Take TAOB. God, we'll need Cody as a pack horse with all this stuff. Kaleen's given the quest an acronym. TAOB: To Adelaide Or Bust. I don't like the bust bit. But it's a good idea, at least if anyone at school overhears us they won't know what we're talking about.

What We Need To Take TAOB

Two changes of clothes, including good clothes for the meeting with Tarrant.

PJs and sleeping bags.

Tent and fold-up chairs.

Pillows.

Blankets.

Ten bottles of water – to be refilled at the saleyards for the trip home.

Toilet paper.

First aid kits. One for humans, one for horses.

Make up and toiletries.

Brushes – horse and human.

Hoof pick.

Two extra Pleasy Boots, one hind, one fore – in case horses cast one.

Two foldable buckets for watering and supplement-feeding horses on the way.

Sunscreen and insect repellent.

iPhones.

Credit cards.

Cash to one hundred dollars – breakfast meeting with Tarrant.

Waterproof pants and jackets.

Twelve kilograms of Working Horse mix.

Small measuring bucket.

Four bags of carrots.

Two bread rolls made up for the first lunch (ham and cheese).

Loaf of bread.

Two packets of biscuits.

Large tube of condensed milk.

Sugar.

Picnic kit with coffee, cups, plates, utensils etc.

Paper towels. Two regular towels.

Four large tins of stew.

Four packets of instant noodles – chicken.

Three bars of chocolate.

Block of cheese.

Freezer packs.

Kerosene burner mini-stove.

Bottle of kerosene.

Liquid hand cleaner.

Small kettle.

Small saucepan.

Face washers.

Toothbrushes and toothpaste.

Torch.

Matches.

Wire cutters.

Sewing kit.

The next two pages were printouts of Google Earth maps: the way TAOB – To Adelaide Or Bust – and estimated time of arrival.

There were weather forecast maps for the next five days. On the last one of these Kaleen had written, 'will update', in red ink. And a page of names of places where we would be stopping for rests. Mostly at public parks in small towns along the way.

The last page had a hand-drawn sketch of the sale yards with a circle, again in red ink, at the back of the sheep pens. She'd also drawn some sheep with dags hanging from their bums and funny expressions on their woolly black faces.

## 17

The following week shoots past in a blur of riding. I've been going on my bike to Kaleen's every afternoon after school, to work Spirit. Also we've been doing more planning for TAOB. However, I keep thinking up reasons why we shouldn't do it. Like there are murderers on the loose. Although that's the least of my concerns. I still think it's Mr Pingelly who's guilty, so I don't really believe we're in any danger. He wouldn't hurt his own daughter. Still, it sounds dramatic. And it did stop Kaleen mid-sentence when I brought it up (I didn't mention her father of course), although she shooed it away with a well worn platitude.

I had been worried we might not have the horses fit enough for the journey, but the way they've been jumping out of their skins lately, they could do it tomorrow and we still have another week before we go.

Kaleen's been working online with Tarrant Moselle, editing her novel and trying to come up with a new title. He does seem to know what he's doing; he's been very helpful and has gone up in my estimation. However, I'm still not sure. I need to see what he looks like. And even if he isn't a monster, it doesn't mean he's perfect. The rest of us are only human.

Anyway, Tarrant knows we're riding to Adelaide, he's the only person we've told, and says he wants to take some pics for future publicity. I don't like this. How would I explain it to the parents? But Kaleen says I don't have to be in the photos, so I guess it's okay. I don't think she cares about her parents finding out. She hasn't even told them about her novel, or how it's going to be published.

Monday rolls around again and Kaleen isn't at school until after lunch. She looks pale and has a strange blue-grey aura. I don't have a chance to talk to her until we're on the bus going home. Even then, it's hard to get any sense out of her. She keeps covering her mouth and whispering so low I can barely hear her. I do make out 'Cops' and 'TAOB', something about that being cancelled. This time, even though the bus pulls up and Mr Tangelo glances my way, I don't get off at my stop.

With Kaleen open-mouthed next to me, I text Mum, saying I'll be going to Kaleen's, and could she pick me up later. I know she's not working shift tonight, so she shouldn't mind. I also text that I'll vacuum the house as well as do all my Saturday work on Friday. We'd already fixed it up with our parentals to stay at each other's places this weekend. We're supposed to be heading TAOB on Saturday morning around six.

Kaleen's still silent as we walk up her driveway. When we get to her house, she grabs my bag and dumps it, with hers, on the front step. Then she drags me off to one of the empty stables.

It's only when we're inside, with the door closed, that she starts to talk. 'Vel, it's terrible. The worst blurry thing. The homicide cops were here last night and took Father away in handcuffs. They've also been questioning all the workers. Even Donovan. Mother's mortified their affair will become public.'

I lean back on the wall, kick over the bedding straw with my foot. I don't know what to say. I don't trust my voice, I know it will sound unsurprised. So I nod and raise my eyebrows.

'They brought Father back this morning. Now he wants to sack Donovan. Donovan's gone off camping with Cody for a few days, and I can't find the saddlebags, so he must have taken them too. Mother and Father screamed at each other all morning. Their worst argument ever. I wasn't going to go to school, but I did in the end. I got one of the other stockmen to take me, just to get away from the noise.'

I touch Kaleen's arm. I still don't trust my voice, but I know I have to say something. 'So, why is this stopping us from going TAOB?'

Kaleen pulls away from me and for a moment I think she's about to do her theatrical act. Maybe fling herself down on the straw.

Then she grabs both my arms and grins. 'You're absolutely right, Vel! Why should this stop us? And it makes it easier. With all this happening, no one's going to notice the horses missing. I'd been wondering how I'd explain to Donovan about taking Cody to your place.' Kaleen looks up at the stable's ceiling.

I look up too and see a huge spider spinning a very intricate web.

Kaleen continues, 'But with Donovan and Cody gone, I don't have to worry. And anyway, Ganny can be our packhorse.'

Now my voice is full. 'Oh hell, Kaleen, not Ganymede. Don't you remember how he was when I rode him to Old Ma Izzy's? Even she told me to be careful.'

Kaleen's lips thin. The blue from her aura has lifted and she's now as grey as steel. I recall how she said quests were supposed to be difficult and hard. I can almost see her mind putting quotations around these thoughts.

Then I hear a familiar toot and an engine which sounds like gravel churning in a cement mixer. I peer out of the stable door and see Mum's old Holden scrunching up the driveway. Saved by the horn, I think, as I scoot out to meet her.

Mum's staring at me weirdly as I climb into the car. I feel a shiver wash through me like a wave. Perhaps she's found out what we're planning to do.

'I'm not sure you should be coming here any more, Vel,' she says. 'Something's going on with the Pingellys. It was bad enough with those two men being murdered. But tonight there's been talk on the news about Kaleen's father being taken in for questioning.'

So that's why she's picked me up early. I look down at my shoes. 'He's back home now, Mum. And they've questioned everyone.' I don't say anything about the handcuffs. Anyway, Kaleen might have been exaggerating.


Tuesday and Wednesday, Kaleen is off school. Kiss is having a great time spreading poison about the Pingellys. I'm disappointed how a lot of kids are going along with it. The whole school is buzzing with rumours. I don't blame Kaleen for not turning up. I wish I could stay home too. Practically everyone's calling me Half-caste now. A feeding frenzy by association. I'm so totally alone, even the most unpopular kid in our class is keeping away from me.

Kiss is also milking the sympathy factor with her broken leg. It's in a bright pink cast and has heaps of signatures, and silly sayings, scrawled all over it. Brandon and Willem Van Den Hoven haven't written on it. I've heard Brandon did well at the Horse Jumping Expo on Sylvania Star. Seems like he has her back on track.

Mum's stopped me from going to Kaleen's so I haven't even been able to exercise Spirit or help Kaleen with Ganny. To make it worse, I've no phone credit left again and I don't get my pocket money until Friday. Also, Kaleen hasn't bothered to ring me. I'm starting to give up on this TAOB thing. The way it's going, it's not going.

Thursday, I'm relieved to see Kaleen sitting on our usual seat on the bus. She moves closer to the window, I slide over next to her and put my bag on the floor. She's looking wild-haired, but sort of grounded too, if that makes sense.

'Everything's going to be okay, Vel. I've been working Spirit off Watson every day, and I found out Ganny's been doing stock work too up until now. Also, being an Arab, he's naturally good at endurance.'

I feel like butting in and saying it's not Ganny's fitness I'm worried about, but I keep quiet and Kaleen continues.

'And I've managed to find some more saddlebags. Got them off Old Ma Izzy. She didn't even ask questions. But Vel,' Kaleen pauses and lowers her already soft voice to a bare whisper, 'I think she knows. As I was leaving, she told me to be careful, and for the Norse Trinity to be with us. Whatever that is.'

Norse Trinity: where had I seen that before? Then I remember. 'Oh, Kaleen, I know what it is. There's a poem above her stove, in a similar frame to her Freya photo one. I read it last time I was there. A couple of times, actually. I really liked it. You and Old Ma Izzy were outside. I'd come in to get some apples as an after-drench treat for the horses.'

I close my eyes, see Old Ma Izzy's immaculate kitchen, her combustion stove and the lovely wooden frame above it with words in calligraphic script. I read them aloud.

Freya
A Norse Trinity stands the time
of spoken word
Thor, Odin, and Freya
Freya, more beautiful than Troy's Helen
Fertility, love, wealth
and warfare
she took those battlefield slain
to Folkvang
to be planted
in her 'field of folk'
Odin has his share buried at Valhalla
And when Viking girls are married
they are given
feline presents to honour Freya
descendants of the cats
who drew her chariot and kept at bay
from palace graves
the rats
that came to gnaw the corn-silked weeds
and shelter in their tombs.

'How did you remember it all?' Kaleen is staring at me and sounds breathless.

I open my eyes, shake my head. 'I'm not sure. It was really strange. I could see it. Like the poem was in my mind. Even the script looked exactly the same.'

Kaleen's eyebrows arch. 'It's a bit dark, Vel, but lovely too.'

I nod and take a deep breath. 'I can't really see how this TAOB is going to happen, Kaleen. You know I'm not allowed over to your place any more. Mum's still worried about everything that's been going on.' My voice is even, but inwardly I'm heartbroken. Mum doesn't know what she's asking me to do. How will I get to be with Spirit? And I love going to Kaleen's.

Kaleen pats my shoulder. 'Don't worry, Vel. I'll come over to your place after school and talk to her. Things will be fine.'

**18**

I can't believe we'll be going TAOB tomorrow! Last night after school, Kaleen talked to Mum. Kaleen sent me out of the room (I went and brushed Sebby) so I don't know what she told her, but it did the trick. Mum seemed different when I came back. And just before I left to go to Kaleen's, Mum took me aside and, with a frown creasing her brow, said how Kaleen might be very rich but she was pretty poor in some ways, and to be nice to her. As if I'm not always nice to Kaleen. It's funny, but I do know what Mum means, especially with what's been going on. I'm hoping TAOB will cheer Kaleen up.

Kaleen's mother knows I'm staying here at their house tonight, but she thinks we're taking the horses to my place first thing tomorrow morning. She did query if it was okay with my dad; she knows how he feels about horses ruining fences and digging up the paddocks.

Kaleen pulls me through her doorway quickly and shuts the door behind us, first glancing down the hallway to make sure no one's around. The floor of her bedroom is littered with supplies; even the bag of horse mix is here. I still have to put my changes of clothes and my jacket into the pile as well.

I suck in a breath. We'll need a wagon to take all this stuff.

Kaleen stands looking at it all with an odd expression on her face and nibbles on her thumbnail. 'I think we may need to cut back on a few things.' She draws out the word 'few'.

I put my hands on my hips. 'More than a few things, Kaleen. Why do we need pillows for a start? We can bundle up the saddle blankets to put under our heads. PJs can go. We can sleep in our T-shirts.'

'Yeah, I was thinking we can cut back on the number of bottles of water too. We'll be making heaps of stops on the way. There's bound to be taps at the parks. Two bottles each should be enough.'

I walk around the room, pushing over items with my toe. 'Some of these things can go in our pockets.' I pick up the sewing kit and the packets of chicken noodles. 'And we can carry lots of stuff in our backpacks.'

Kaleen puts on her convincing face. Screwed-up serious. 'You know, Donovan's saddlebags were heaps bigger than these ones. I think they're too small.' She indicates the leather saddlebags propped against the wall.

I ignore answering. 'If we halve up the working horse mix into six kilos a bag, it will balance the load better and there'll still be room for things on top. It means unpacking when we want to give the horses a snack, but it can't be helped.'

Kaleen's eyes brighten. 'Hey, Ganny's load will get lighter the further we travel and we'll have extra space.'

'We can lighten our backpacks then,' I say. 'So, no more excuses, let's get TAOB on the road!'

Kaleen smiles, and pushes my shoulder. 'Vel,' she says, being overly logical on purpose, 'we're not going till tomorrow.'

We slip into a sort of mime, holding things up to each other and nodding, or shaking our heads. It's not long before the To Go pile is smaller, but still much bigger than the Leaving Behind pile.

Before we creep into our bunk beds, we set the alarms on our watches, survey the neatly packed backpacks and bulging saddlebags, and grin.

I pull the sheet up around my chin and, half in a dream, ask Kaleen how Ganny had gone wearing the saddlebags for the first time. She doesn't answer. How can she be asleep already? I feel like I'm going to stay awake all night.

I lie back, listen to all things country outside the window. The noise of crickets and the soft neighs and stamping of the horses in their stables drift into the room on the night air.

It seems no time at all before our watches are shrilling. It's five a.m. already. We scrabble beneath the sheets to turn them off.

'Right, Vel, you start taking everything outside. Put it all next to the tack shed. I'll give the horses a light breakfast. Then we'll have ours.' She's off as soon as she utters the words and as she heads outside I see she's already dressed. She must have slept in her clothes.

I get dressed, pack our lunch and choose what gear I'm taking out first. The horses will need an hour to eat and to let it digest, so we have plenty of time to do it all. We can brush and saddle them after they've eaten, and the Pleasy Boots only take a few minutes to slip on.

The only hiccup we have is Coral Lee arriving home with her lovesick boyfriend, Dwayne. She and Kaleen exchange a few words. Coral Lee's not convinced we're just going to my place. Not with all this gear and food. Kaleen manages to call a truce. Coral Lee won't tell on us and we won't tell on her for breaking her curfew. The latest Coral Lee is supposed to be home is twelve-thirty.

Ganymede is surprisingly good with the saddlebags. It turns out Kaleen has had them on him before, but not loaded up of course. He's a bit funny with us putting on his nearside hind Pleasy Boot, but several carrots do the trick. Eventually he stamps sharply into it and we clip it on. Although he's snorting, fidgeting and looking sideways, Kaleen keeps saying he'll get quieter when the sun comes up. What is he? A vampire?

The updated weather maps Kaleen has printed out say the weekend is going to be fine, with cold nights. It's well into autumn now, so that figures.

Somewhere near, a mopoke calls its sad short syllables and one of the other stock horses whinnies out to Ganymede, who stretches low his neck and whinnies back. It's shrill and piercing. I look over to the house but no one's stirring. All the lights are off.

'You're just saying bye to your paddock mate, Topper, aren't you, Ganny?' Kaleen says, handing Ganny another carrot and scratching his withers.

The other horses move up to Kaleen and she gives them a carrot each as well.

I take the rest of the bag from her (five carrots less for me to carry), slip it into my backpack and swing aboard Spirit. He shifts his weight, but doesn't move forward until I give him the signal. I'm to go in front, as

Kaleen has to lead Ganny and wants to keep him to the side of her, away from the traffic. When we can, we'll go three abreast with me and Spirit on the outside.

The air is crisp and breezeless with the still dark new morning and we walk alongside Dwayne, not talking as he slinks back to his car. He's left it parked at an angle right across the Pingellys' gateway.

I can hear the rumble of the main road and smell the faint fumes of petrol and diesel. The semi-trailers, commuters and tradies are on the move already.

Out along the verge, we push the horses into a working trot. Their ears are forward and their tails are up. Kaleen and I look at each other and smile. Finally TAOB is on its way!

# 19

After an hour of riding, the sun is beginning to rise and I'm looking for signs that Ganny will calm down. He either keeps rushing forward on the lead rope, ahead of Watson, or hanging back so that Kaleen has her arm outstretched in a manner which looks excruciating. But she doesn't complain. The excitement of us going TAOB is carrying the momentum and lifting our mood.

The paddocks on either side of the main road are flooded with golden light, the drying grass glints silver and every now and then sheep and cattle look up or follow us along like fellow travellers, until a fence stops their progress.

At first we talked in a flurry, but now with the sunshine warming our thoughts we drift into silence, smiling occasionally at each other, or indicating with lifted reins when we want to trot, or dropping the reins down on the horses' necks when we want to walk.

Kaleen is the first to say something. 'You know, Vel, it's all working to plan.' She glances at her watch. 'If we keep up this pace, we'll be at our first stop in half an hour.'

I feel like shouting at her, 'Oh, god, Kaleen, you should never tempt fate.' Life has taught me this: complacency has no place for words. Think it by all means, but don't make it audible.

I slip a look behind me, see nothing in the distance but seemingly endless verge and an SUV with its lights still on. Maybe everything will be okay.

We make our first stop at a roadside park and toilet block a few kilometres from town. It's all so familiar to me. This is the route we take to school. In fact, we'll be going past there soon.

'Gee, Kaleen. We're nearly faster than the school bus.'

Kaleen laughs. 'Well,' she says, 'we don't have Spider Johnson aboard.'

A man comes out of the toilet shaking water, or worse, from his hands. Ganny jumps, pulls backwards, and Kaleen quickly winds his lead rope around her pommel to take the strain. Watson's wearing a Western saddle too, today. We wait until the guy has driven off before dismounting.

Kaleen consults her notes. 'Only a short rest stop here. Give the horses a few carrots and we'll have a pee and be on our way.'

I almost feel like saluting and saying, 'Yes, sir,' but I giggle instead.

Kaleen's rubbing her shoulder. She stretches her fingers and closes and opens her hand.

'Do you want me to lead Ganny for a while?' I say. 'Give your arm a break?'

Kaleen looks up sharply then giggles too. 'I should be okay for a bit longer,' she says, her voice high. 'I'll hand him over when I get tired.'

We set off at a trot. Watson keeps dashing ahead of us every time Ganny surges forward. In the end, I let them go in front but keep to their side, nearest the road. When Ganny hangs back, I can see him looking over his shoulder and showing the whites of one eye, like he's being followed. One thing which is good, though, he's shown no fear of the trucks or cars. We even had the double-decker city bus go past, running late judging by the speed it was doing. Ganny didn't flicker a forelock.

After another hour of riding, I'm wondering when Ganny will settle down. Kaleen handed him over to me about fifteen minutes ago and I don't know how she's been putting up with it. My arm's aching already. I've tried tug and release, but he's no better. He seems to be pulling back more often. And the hills, which loom up every few kilometres or so, give him extra excuses for slowing down.

Suddenly he twists round, stops dead and gives out a huge neigh, his body quivering from tip to tail. My arm is wrenched and I swear black and colours but manage to wind the rope around my pommel. Spirit neighs out too and Watson follows suit. When all three horses look backwards, we look back as well. We've just come around a bend and we can't hear any traffic, but there's a strange hum, a sort of collective whir behind us on the road, and it's getting louder.

Ganny leaps forward just as a brown blur of legs and tail gallops up alongside. It's Ganny's paddock mate, Topper, oozing blood from a long pencil-thin gash across his chest and shoulders. A strand of barbed wire is tangled in his mane and he's puffing like a dragon. Ganny sprints forward, but Spirit, obviously remembering his calf-roping days, plants his feet and the lead rope twangs to its end.

The hum is getting closer. I grab another look and draw in a breath.

A flash of cyclists, riding in a peloton, come skimming past in a psychedelic blur of lycra. I catch a glimpse of Brandon and Willem in the lead positions. They glance back, under their arms, and I know they've seen us.

This sucks. This really sucks! Why do they keep catching us in such bloody embarrassing situations?

Kaleen gets off Watson, removes his halter, and loops his reins around her arm. She takes a carrot from her pocket and talks quietly but firmly as she approaches the runaway. 'Oh, look at you, Topper. You silly old boy. Got yourself all tangled up.' Without looking at me, she calls back, 'Vel, can you get the wire cutters? They're in the saddlebags. Left-hand side pocket. And get the first aid kit too.'

Ganymede is fidgeting and pulling on his rope, trying to get closer to the other horse. A classic case of separation anxiety.

Kaleen leads Topper over to us. Ganny visibly loosens, lets out an extended puff and nickers softly. The four horses touch noses, the equivalent of an equine group hug. Then they stiffen, heads up, ears forward. Spirit is the first to relax.

In the distance, but coming closer, I see Brandon and Willem riding back towards us at a sedate pace. Their wheels are catching the sun in their spokes. And with only the two of them, the whir is much softer.

Kaleen snips off the barbed wire, untangles it carefully and puts it into her backpack. It's just a short piece. She takes out some antiseptic from the horse first-aid kit, and quickly sprays it across the thin furrowed wound. It doesn't need stitches. Topper quivers for a second, then stands still.

Kaleen's staring at the ground when Brandon swings off his bike.

'Hi, girls.' Brandon points at Topper. 'We saw this one kilometres ago, going like a werewolf had his heels.'

Willem comes closer and rubs Topper's shoulder. 'What's de story we're having here, ladies?' Willem's accent is lovely, his voice chocolate.

For the first time, I really look at him. He's quite tall, about half a head above Brandon. But slimmer. His hair is lighter, his face chiselled. Not handsome but interesting.

Kaleen and I exchange glances. I wait for her to talk first. After all, it is her quest. In the end, she tells them we're heading to Adelaide, for her book deal signing.

Both guys lift their eyebrows and whistle.

'And Velvet?'

He knows my name. Willem touches my arm and I feel a tingle like an electric shock.

'Why too, is she going?'

I'm praying Kaleen doesn't blab about my ability in a moment of lustful distraction. She still hasn't been able to meet Brandon's eyes.

'Velvet's my agent. We'll be camping at the sale yards near the city. We have a meeting with my publisher on Sunday morning at the Best Arms Hotel.'

God, Kaleen, I think, why don't you just tell them everything? Then I realise she more or less has. And Brandon's probably already guessed our parents don't know what we're doing.

'Right.' Brandon cups his chin. 'Seems to me you girls could do with a little help. I figure you weren't intending for this interloper to come along.'

Kaleen looks at Topper and then at the ground again and scuffs the dirt with her boot.

For a minute, no one speaks.

'Tell you what. Bring him to my place. It's just up the road. You can leave him there and pick him up on your way back tomorrow. I'll put him in a stable. Can't have him getting out again. Although by the look of it, he's not much of a jumper. Good thing his hinds didn't get caught. Vicious stuff, barbed wire.'

I hand Ganymede back to Kaleen and take Topper's lead rope. The guys zoom off like eagles on their racing bikes and we nearly have to gallop to keep up. Luckily, the horses on the leads stay with us and don't hang back.

About a kilometre up the road, we turn off into a winding driveway. Two gothic-looking gates bar our way. Brandon points a remote control at them and they slide open. We all pass through and the doors glide shut behind us. OMG, Brandon's place really rocks.

In the avenue leading up to his house, high fronded trees meet, hanging over in a green canopy. Brandon's mansion makes Kaleen's home look like a cottage.

I don't know much about gardens, but this is stunning as well. Colours of white and gold are eye-closing with their brilliance. Standard roses seem to be the main feature, set off with underpinnings of other things in various stages of alchemy. I draw in a breath and cast a sideways look at Kaleen, but she seems to be in a gloom again.

<h1 style="text-align:center">20</h1>

Half an hour later, we're on our way once more. We've had to leave Ganny behind at Brandon's along with Topper. Ganny put up even more of a fight when we tried to leave Topper there. His nervousness was affecting Spirit and Watson as well. I guess they were thinking it was about time to go home, and with Topper calling out like a demon possessed and Ganny trying to bolt backwards on his lead line, I don't blame them.

Brandon and Willem are ace, though. Not only have they given up their ride today with their cycling group for us, but Brandon was the one to suggest we leave Ganymede there with Topper when he saw Kaleen having so much trouble with him.

Repacking has been a hassle, though.

Spirit and Watson are calming down with every kilometre we travel. We've been silent; we don't want to talk up trouble, tempt fate, like saying how good things are going.

Finally Kaleen speaks. 'I'm not sure we should let the guys help us, Vel,' she says quietly, slowing Watson from a trot to a walk.

Spirit nudges Watson with his nose, and Watson snorts. It's almost like they're sharing a private joke. Probably about us. I don't feel like joining in. We're about an hour off schedule and our backpacks are so loaded I can hardly lift my shoulders and, as far as TAOB being a secret is concerned, well, that's been shredded. Old Ma Izzy knows, Coral Lee and her dozy boyfriend Dwayne know, and now Brandon and Willem are in on it too.

'We have to, Kaleen. There's no way we can take all the stuff ourselves.'

Brandon had offered to drop off our sleeping bags, the tent and some of the food at the sale yards later today. He didn't say how they'd get there. Most probably one of their workmen will bring them.

'The only thing is, Vel, I don't like someone we don't know knowing about us. I mean, Coral Lee won't tell, not with what I have on her. And I'm not just talking about her coming home late this morning. Old Ma Izzy, we know she's fine, and Brandon and Willem, they're on our side as well.'

'I wouldn't worry, Kaleen. I'm sure Brandon will be careful what he tells the workmen.'

Kaleen pushes Watson into a slow canter, and glances back at me. 'It's not only that, Vel. Quests are supposed to be difficult. I don't like to take the easy way out. Maybe we should have persevered. Taken Topper to be our packhorse. He's usually a sensible old boy. He's never ever tried to jump out before. I guess he's been feeling insecure with Cody gone.'

I squeeze Spirit into a canter and pull level with Kaleen. 'Ganymede may be missing Cody too, Kaleen. Which would explain why he's become so attached to Topper and why they're so dependent on each other. Watson's fine, he's always been a loner, well, ever since Holmsey…' I stop talking for a second. 'Anyway, Watson has Spirit now. And they're great mates as well. Aren't you, boys?' I lean over and ruffle Watson's mane, then I scratch Spirit's withers so he won't feel left out.

When we drop back to a walk again, Kaleen takes two slivers of carrot from her pocket and gives a piece to each horse. 'We need to stop in two hours. Give them a rest,' she says, wiping her hands on her jeans.

In the next little town, we have an audience, several families with young kids having a picnic in the park. They ask what the horses' names are and if they can pat them. I tell them rubbing or scratching is best and I show them where the horses like it the most. We're certainly leaving a trail of witnesses if the coppers want to follow us.

We take the saddles off the horses and give them a rub down, mostly drying off the sweat around the ears and saddle and girth area. We offer them buckets of water and then some of the working horse mix. Thank goodness – two kilos less to carry.

After they've scoffed the feed, they both roll on the ground and then begin eating the grass. Kaleen and I take it in turns to go to the toilet. Afterwards we collapse on the lawn next to the horses, but keep a firm hold on their lead ropes.

Kaleen gets out our packed lunch, the two bread rolls I made this morning with thick slices of cheese and ham. We finish by scoffing half a block of chocolate and wash it all down with a long drink of water.

'What do you think of Willem, Kaleen?' I say, gazing up at the sky, watching a cloud lazily drift by as lonely as that famous poem.

'Mm, okay, I suppose.' Her voice sounds strange. 'Vel,' she says, voicing what she must have been thinking, 'I still reckon we've taken the easy way out.'

'Hell, Kaleen. This is hardly easy. Anyway, who said quest travellers can't ask for outside help? As long as it's not from the olds.'

'Old Ma Izzy is old,' Kaleen says.

'No, she's not. She's cool. You know what I mean, Kaleen. Parents and all those others who wouldn't understand. Those sort of olds. Not really an age but a quality.'

'Geez, Vel.' Kaleen laughs. 'Quests certainly bring out your philosophical side. I agree with you, though. Old Ma Izzy is way cool.'

Watson comes dangerously close to standing on my foot. These Pleasy Boots may be great to lessen concussion on the road, but they don't soften a hard hoof when it treads on you.

I slide back. 'Watch out, Watson, you big oaf,' I mutter.

He ignores me, puffs breath into the grass and noisily rips off some more juicy shoots. It sounds like grass Velcro.

'We need to make tracks soon,' Kaleen says, looking at her watch.

She gets up, brushes leaves and grass from her jeans and then starts on Watson with the curry comb. Round circular movements. Watson lowers his head and does several long blinks. Spirit stops eating, narrow-eyes him and moves closer to me.

'I'll borrow that after you, Kaleen. When you've finished.'

Ten minutes later, we're TAOB again. We ride for the next two hours, then get off and walk. The horses seem fine, still stepping out and only lightly sweating.

Kaleen wipes a hand over her forehead. 'I think the horses are doing much better than we are,' she says, mirroring my thoughts.

The verge along here is sandy and uneven. I stumble, feel the sun burning into my neck as my hard hat slips forward.

I see Kaleen having trouble too. 'Difficult enough for you, then?'

Kaleen grins at me, and nods. She brings out a bottle of water and takes a swig. Then she shifts her backpack, opens the slot on the front and removes her map. 'About another hour, then we can rest again. We need to get the horses up to some sort of pace which won't wear them out but will cover the ground. I want to make the sale yards before dark.'

'Could let them jog,' I say, lifting my backpack onto Spirit's saddle.


Traffic has slowed. It's mid-afternoon. Sightseers and caravans keep going past with regular monotony. Sometimes a car will slow down to a crawl. Being cautious, I suppose, but having no idea about horses. Our horses couldn't give a horseshoe toss, but a young horse like Zeus, the new colt Old Ma Izzy has started, would see it as predatory.

'I'm sure that's the same car which passed us a while ago,' Kaleen says to a departing SUV, which has now got up to speed.

'Can't be. We never saw it coming back.'

Kaleen shrugs. 'The heat's getting to me. Let's stop over there, under those trees, have a break.'

We let the horses eat some of the grass. Because of the sand, it's short, although, if the horses' faces are anything to go by, delicious.

'It might have doubled back when we stopped at the town. We weren't on the main road then.'

'What are you talking about, Kaleen? Oh, the SUV? Anyway, what makes you think it's the same one?'

'Tinted windows. I couldn't see in. That weird bull-bar. And the colour, grey, I remember thinking it almost camouflaged with the road. I was wondering if the colour of a car makes for safety. I was also thinking they don't know much about horses.'

I hitch up my backpack and haul myself into the saddle. Spirit stands patiently.

'It's not the only car which has slowed down, Kaleen. Did you get its number plate?'

'Only the letters. I made up an acronym.' Kaleen swings aboard Watson and straightens her pack. 'Stupid Wanker Guy. SWG.'

'SWG. Fair enough,' I say, irrationally hoping he's not related to Hanker Wanker. I push Spirit into a jog. Kaleen comes up alongside. The road is shimmering mirages; it reminds me I'm thirsty. I take out my water bottle, have a drink and offer it to Kaleen. She downs the rest in big gulps. I don't mind, I have another bottle.

It's getting on into the afternoon and the sun is no longer directly above us.

In the distance ahead, I see a vehicle bearing towards us at great speed. It's gunmetal grey and looks exactly like the SUV that just passed us. My mind is whirring, but everything else is going in slow motion, like you read in books.

I yell out to Kaleen the one word, 'Gallop!' I dig my heels in hard.

Spirit jumps into high gear and pig-roots at the sudden insult, the first time he's ever done that. My backpack slips up on my shoulders, but the acceleration of the gallop pushes it down. I take a deep breath, steer Spirit straight ahead. I'm still watching the approaching car. It's on the wrong side of the road now, flashing its lights and close enough to read the letters of its number plate. My heart's thumping my chest like it wants to escape. And I agree with it. Watson and Kaleen are coming up behind us.

For only the second time in my life, I hear Kaleen swear. 'Shit, Vel. SWG!'

I have a quick chance to scream, 'Remember the stampede!' before the car has gone off the road and is bouncing and skidding along the verge towards us.

Another clump of trees is up ahead, no more than a hundred metres. I lift my reins and Spirit hits top gear. Quarter horses are known for acceleration and we're there in seconds. If Kaleen has heard me, she'll know what to do.

The SUV, with its huge bull-bar shaped like steer horns, is so close I could have seen the driver's eyes if it hadn't been for the heavy window tint. I bring Spirit back to a canter and guide him in an arc. The car is careering in the sand towards us. Watson has caught up and I can see Kaleen's face. She's smiling. And I know she's heard me. We weave the horses through the trees and slow down. The car can't fit between them. It roars around to the other side of the trees to cut us off but we double back away from them. It revs its engine and tries to reverse. Now its wheels are spinning up dirt, its motor's screaming and it's spewing black smoke.

'Come on, Kaleen,' I yell. 'I think he might be bogged. Let's bounce!'

In a strange sort of reality, but with the same certainty I had when I was seeing Old Ma Izzy's poem in my mind, I know exactly where we have to go. Both horses leap into action. Galloping full speed in micro seconds. Spirit's in the lead, the grass beneath us a blur, tears sting my eyes from the wind we are creating.

The action beneath me is so smooth, almost like a straight line, and there up ahead, like I knew it would be, is a narrow dirt lane winding off the verge. Huge ghost gums flank both sides and its surface is pockmarked with holes and stones. I can hear the car, but something tells me not to look back. I need to concentrate. Spirit dodges the rocks and leaps over the holes and the mini earthquake-like gashes. The lane curves a bend, and for a moment I can't hear Watson. Then, through a clearing to one side, but hidden by vines, is an opening. Only horse-sized. I dive Spirit through the gap as I scream out for Kaleen. I glance over my shoulder, sigh relief. She's coming through behind me.

<h1 style="text-align:center">21</h1>

The lane goes on and on until there's another gate. A gate without fences. We draw the horses to a trot and jump over the broken rails and rotten posts on one side of it. Fifty metres ahead, we see a house snared in vines, the windows boarded up with shutters and nails. Grass grows thickly around several apple trees with burdens so heavy their branches touch the ground.

'Oh, Kaleen, where are we?' I moan, as I slide off. I can't believe I still have my pack. My feet sting when I hit the ground and the muscles along my spine seem to have disappeared. Even as I say these words, I know we're where we're meant to be. I know we're safe. Perhaps it's the Dreaming. My ancestral connection to the land.

Anyway, an SUV couldn't follow us here. The entrance is too narrow. But he, or they, may be coming on foot, so we don't have time to waste. And we need to be quiet.

On the side of the house there is a huge barn, and when we investigate, we find a smaller shed tacked onto the back of it, with a door almost hidden among the same vines which seem to be smothering the house. Kaleen gets out the wire cutters and we snip pieces of it away until we can scrape open the door. The shed is empty except for a black-hooded buggy festooned in cobwebs, and some cracked leather harness hanging from overhead beams.

Spirit and Watson give short snorts but walk in easily. They're dripping sweat and still puffing like racehorses after a steeplechase. Their skin flickers tiny tremors across the long muscles of their shoulders and hindquarters, and there's flecked white foam between their legs and down their necks. When we're inside the shed, they stand as still as stone, heads down, sides heaving and noses almost touching the dirt floor.

I pull the door closed behind us, glad of the many gaps in the walls and roof which let in a thin light.

I rub Spirit's forehead, just above his eye where he likes it best. He leans towards me and his front legs tremble.

'Oh, Kaleen. They're both exhausted.' I keep my voice low. 'The poor buggers. Weren't they bloody amazing, though?'

Kaleen undoes Watson's girth. 'More than amazing, Vel. They were totally awesome.' She slips off Watson's saddle and takes a deep breath. 'But who the blurry heck was that? What do you think they were trying to do?'

'I don't know, Kaleen, but I wasn't going to hang around to find out. I think he was trying to ram us, or at the least run us into the fence, the bastard. I was way relieved when you knew what I meant when I yelled, "Remember the stampede."'

Kaleen smiles at me. 'How could I forget?'

She was referring to an incident many years ago. I'd been helping Kaleen bring some cows into the yards. I was only eight and it was the first time I'd done it. We weren't on horseback and, when three of the cows had raced towards me with their heads down and looks of intent I was sure weren't good for my health etched on their bovine faces, I'd screamed 'Stampede' and dived behind some trees.

They divided harmlessly around me and, by the time they'd regrouped and turned round, I'd scrambled over the fence to safety. Kaleen had nearly died laughing. Afterwards, she told me it was the funniest thing she had ever seen. They were only poddy calves after a feed, and wouldn't have hurt me, although it didn't feel like that at the time. But my strategy back then had certainly paid off now.

'We need to find some water soon and give the horses a drink. After they've cooled down of course,' Kaleen says softly.

I take out the collapsible buckets from my backpack and unload the torch. 'Looks like we won't be getting to Adelaide tonight.' I'm whispering too.

I hear Kaleen's breath, a sharp intake, like a whistle. 'But what about Brandon and Willem, Vel? They've got our tent and sleeping bags. Not to mention our dinner. It's going to get down to seven degrees tonight.' She chews a fingernail. 'I suppose I could text them.'

'Well, Kaleen, you wanted a proper quest. You know what they say about being careful what you wish for.'

Even in the dull light I can see Kaleen's face aglow.

'Oh, I don't mind really.' There's a ring of truth to her voice as she says it.

I have to admit it is exciting, in a terrifying sort of way. But not if anything happens to the horses. And what the hell were those men up to?

Pulling off Spirit's saddle, I put on a sober tone. 'It's bloody serious, Kaleen. Spirit and Watson could have been hurt back there.'

Kaleen drops her head, sits down on her saddle. Rubs her eyes. When she looks up, her gaze is steady and her next words come out with cold conviction. 'When we find out who has done this, they will pay.' For a moment, she sounds like her woman detective in *Bitter the Taste of Murder*.

Ten minutes later, we hear a rustling noise and freeze. We stretch our hearing for footsteps or voices. But soon we see the culprit. A large grass-bedraggled rat has emerged from under the horse buggy. He sits, eyeing us, head to one side, whiskers flickering, and then without concern he slips beneath the buggy, his tail marking a line in the dust behind him.

We start to laugh but it chokes in our throats. We can hear two loud voices. Coming our way. Definitely male.

Kaleen and I clutch each other. We look at the horses, pray they won't move or make a sound. They've lifted their heads and are listening too, ears wavering.

'Are you sure the brats came this way?'

'Cheeldren go up zis lane. I'm positive.' The second man has an accent, not as nice as Willem's, though.

'I couldn't see. Hard enough to keep the bloody car on the road. Bloody little mongrels. Let's check out this barn. They can't be in the house. It's all boarded up.'

'Hard to be hiding ze horses.'

'Well, I'm fucken pissed off.'

One of them bangs loudly on the tin.

'Wouldn't be doing babysitting duties if it wasn't for that meddling old woman.'

The voices recede and then we hear the men in the barn at the front, moving things. What sounds like someone climbing the rungs of a metal ladder rings out like a metronome. And more cursing. Then there's complete silence.

My arms feel paralysed and my fingers are locked onto Kaleen's arms. I don't think I can let go. What if they look behind the barn and find this shed? Kaleen's face is sheet white and her breath inaudible.

The silence continues.

'I think they've gone.' I can hardly hear my own voice.

 Kaleen lets go of me, an arm at a time. I do the same.

'What did he mean by that meddling old woman?' Kaleen whispers. 'Could it be Old Ma Izzy?'

'Shit, Kaleen. I hope she's all right. Did she say anything to you when you picked up the saddlebags?'

'Only about the Norse Trinity. Hang on, she did mention she'd told J.D. Claridge about our body hunt. How Odin had picked up the scent trail from my place.'

I sit quietly. I can't trust myself to speak. I can't believe it, even of a Category One. To hurt their own child. But what do I know? Parents do kill their kids. You'd see it sometimes on the TV news.

Finally I speak. 'Don't you think it was a bit odd? The scent trail, I mean?'

Kaleen grabs my arms again, but mine won't move. Her voice comes out in a slow drawl. 'No, not...at the...time. But now...I'm not sure what it means.'

I feel like saying, 'Come on, Kaleen, you're the crime writer. The trail starts at your place. The bodies are found nearby. Police come snooping around. Take your father away. Question all the workers.' But even as these thoughts form, it doesn't seem quite right.

Kaleen releases my arms and stands up. 'Anyway, let's get these horses watered. I'm sure those guys have gone, and we can't sit here all day. We do have a quest.'

She appears fully recovered, but then she is a wonderful actress. I also notice she's not calling the quest TAOB any more. I never did like the 'Or Bust' bit.

We're super-careful leaving the shed. With each scrape of the door, we hold our breath. But as we emerge and check everything out, our shoulders loosen and we relax a little. It makes sense they've gone. I mean, they didn't even know for sure we were here. And thank goodness the Pleasy Boots left no horseshoe prints on the hard ground.

There's a tap attached to an old hose near the apple trees. We run the water for what seems like ages, until it looks less rusty, and then fill our buckets. When we get back into the shed, the horses have rolled. Spirit's no longer white but Watson doesn't look too bad. After all, he was brown to begin with.

'Good,' Kaleen says, seemingly to herself, and I know she's planning something.

While the horses finish their fourth bucket of water each, we do a reconnaissance. There's a small yard around the house and we prop up the fences and tie them together with some binder twine we found in the big barn. When we lead Spirit and Watson out there, they lighten up like they've gone to horse heaven.

Watson checks out the fence line, rolls again, and starts cropping the long grass. Spirit nuzzles the gate, lips the knots in the binder twine, and rattles the chain that I'd got from the gate with no fences. He gazes longingly at the apple trees and then at me. I get the hint and fill up one of the buckets. It doesn't take long, there are so many apples. I scatter them over the grass and both horses quickly follow the tumbling treats, like a treasure hunt. Soon happy crunching can be heard. Apple juice froths from their mouths in testament to their enjoyment. They snort and lay their ears back at each other in friendly rivalry every time they go for the same apple. Horsey happiness at its best.

When they finish, they race around the yard and even kick up their heels before getting down to some serious grass eating.

Kaleen unfolds her arms from where she's been leaning on the top of the gate. 'So much for them being tired,' she says, smiling.

I head back to the shed and our supplies. 'I could kill for a cup of coffee,' I say.

This time nothing stops us from laughing.

The one-burner kerosene stove is wonderful and it's only minutes before I have the little kettle boiling away. I put a long squirt of condensed milk into two cups and two heaped teaspoons of instant coffee as well. The rest of the chocolate has melted and we place the gooey wrapper under the buggy for the rat to have for dinner, or a late lunch, whatever his mealtime preference.

We're starving, so we quickly scoff a whole packet of YoYo biscuits between us. I pull out my iPhone, try ringing the guys, but there's no signal here. We lean back against one of the apple trees and look at the horses eating.

Kaleen glances at her watch, gets out her map printout, and starts scribbling something at the bottom of the page.

I've learnt the hard way never to interrupt Kaleen when she's writing. So I wait, try to distract myself by following some ants carrying bits of YoYo biscuit twice as big as themselves. They're on a quest as well. A survival quest. Maybe we are too. I shiver.

'You're not cold are you, Vel?'

I shake my head.

Kaleen stops writing, chews her pen. Thumps the grass with a closed fist. 'Right, this is how I see it. It's six-thirty. The guys, and whoever has taken them, probably would have dropped off our gear by now. It'll be dark soon. The horses have had heaps to eat and a good rest. You saw them bucking around. They're fine. I've calculated we're just over an hour's ride from the sale yards. We can still make it.'

I peer at Kaleen to see if she's joking. But the more I think about it, the more it makes sense. Only one thing I'm worried about. I touch Kaleen's arm. 'What about those men, Kaleen? What if they're waiting for us?'

'That's why we're going under the cover of darkness, Vel,' she says, her voice low. 'I was bit concerned before about Spirit and his brighter than bright white, but he's fixed that by rolling. Don't brush him. Well, maybe just where the saddle goes.'

We return to the shed.

As Kaleen goes to walk through the door, I grab her by the elbow. 'Don't move,' I hiss.

A brown, sleek snake with a pale yellow belly is sliding over the threshold. We follow it in at a distance and watch as it slinks, tongue flicking, beneath the old horse buggy. The snake too, has left a line in the dust, but this one is wavy.

When we hear a squeal, I feel shivery all over, even though it's still warm. 'Poor rat,' I say. 'Dinner time for the snake, I think.'

Kaleen is trembling. 'I hate snakes.' Her words crack a little. 'I hope the rat at least got to eat a bit of the chocolate.'

We go further into the shed and rush our gear outside. Now I'm super-pleased we don't have to sleep there like I'd thought we'd have to.

We get the horses saddled right on dusk. The shadows are lengthening and the trees are turning dark, even the apple ones. I pick another apple for each of the horses and one for us as well, to eat on the way.

We set off at a walk, let the horses get into stride, then push them into a working trot. It's not very long before we're on the main road again. We keep to the fence line and, when the dusk light fades to nightness, I get out the torch and shine a narrow beam onto the path in front of us.

Kaleen knows the way really well; she's been Google Earthing it for weeks. We easily find the bike track, which will help us avoid the busiest roads.

The Pleasy Boots excel on the tarmac. And they don't make much sound, so we won't be heard. Not that the SUV could follow us here anyway.

I pull up alongside Watson, and Spirit matches his pace so we're neck to neck.

'Where do you think that man's accent was from, Kaleen?'

'Not sure. It wasn't Dutch. He didn't sound like Willem. Maybe French? Or Italian?'

The track takes us across a bridge over a bypass. I look down at the traffic speeding along like shiny metallic beasts.

Then back on the road, up ahead, at last we see the sale yards. They're lit up with fluorescent lights on high poles. I can see sheep milling around in low pens and a row of high wooden yards with brown and white cattle, shoulder to rump. Herefords. Those poddy calves that had chased me were Herefords. There are other yards containing slightly smaller black cattle: Angus. Kaleen told me if you breed Hereford with Angus you get what the cattlemen call Mickey Mouse offspring, with the classic black and white faces.

Kaleen has ridden up ahead and is standing to one side of the entrance. In the light I can see the rest of our gear in a strapped-up heap by one of the gates. I look around. Wonder how long it was since the guys were here.

Kaleen dismounts and, still hanging onto Watson's reins, collapses gracefully to her knees. She covers her eyes with her free hand. 'Fricken heck,' she wails. 'There's not supposed to be a shirty market on today.'

I look at the noticeboard. 'You're right about that, Kaleen. It isn't. It's tomorrow. Starts seven-thirty. First up, fat lambs and yearlings.'

Kaleen slumps down further. 'Well, we can't camp here, then. No spare pens, and the place will be crowded with buyers in the morning.'

I dismount, join Kaleen on the ground. The horses let out simultaneous sighs and snort down their noses at us. They sound fed-up.

There's no way we can go home tonight. But we can't stay here. Not with these sale yard lights shining on us like beacons, and all the pens and yards taken.

I stand and pull Kaleen up. 'Come on, Kaleen. You gotta see the good side. We got here. We made it! We made TAOB!'

Kaleen swallows heavily, she's staring behind me. I turn in time to see two headlights approaching noiselessly. The vehicle must be in neutral, with its engine off. My stomach swirls and I feel colder than I did when I thought of that snake devouring the poor rat.

<h1 style="text-align:center">23</h1>

A familiar voice rings out. 'Hey, you ladies. You in trouble again?' It's Willem. The 'vehicle' turns out to be the guys riding two abreast, cycle lights ablaze.

In the white light, I can see Kaleen's colour rising back to her face. Later, she'll probably try to convince me she knew it was Brandon and Willem all along.

The guys are on mountain bikes. They look like heavy-duty racing ones. They have 'Scott' white-printed down their frames as well, exactly like their road racing bikes. But even I can tell the difference.

Brandon has a huge backpack like the ones you see carried by serious bushwalkers. There are water bottles hanging from its sides and two rolled-up sleeping bags strapped on top. Not ours. Willem must have carried our gear.

'We've just been to the shops. Got here an hour ago. Figured we must have beaten you. Thought we would.' Brandon chuckles. 'And we didn't even get going until three.'

Kaleen's face goes red. I grab her arm. Stop her words with mine. I feel shitty too. But the guys don't know.

I force my voice clear and crisp. 'We've had some trouble. A bloody SUV tried to run us off the verge. We had to hole up in an abandoned house.'

Brandon looks at me with interest. 'Wow, way cool.'

Willem's brow creases. 'Dis is not cool, Bran. De ladies could have been injured.'

Brandon shrugs off his backpack. 'You don't know this one.' He points at Kaleen. 'She can look after herself. Don't you worry about that. She took no prisoners on the show circuit.'

Willem screws up his face. 'No prisoners? Oh,' he says, and laughs. 'I see your meaning.'

They're both staring at Kaleen and I feel pissed off that I haven't been included. But Brandon doesn't know me. Anyway, being this close to him is enough. OMG, he's so hot. And Willem is intriguing too. Even in this artificial light he has the most unusual aura. A colour I can't define.

Kaleen has calmed down, mollified, I think, by Brandon's last comment. We tell the guys our other problem. They're not concerned. They tell us there's a truck and vehicle rest stop about a kilometre away; we can put up there. Willem offers to carry our stuff again.

As we ride away together, Willem says, 'So many sheeps. Poor tings. And all de little cows.'

I love his accent. The guys are in front of us so I have the time, and visual aspect, to check out their butts. I see Kaleen checking them out as well. So hot they make Lycra look cool.

When we get to the rest stop, Brandon tells us that Willem has something to say. He waves his hand in Willem's direction.

Willem carefully places our tent and other gear on the ground up against the fence, and faces us. 'Ladies, I have a proposal. We should not be leaving you on your alone. I say to Brandon before we come, we should be bringing our camping gear too.'

So that's why Brandon had his huge backpack. And the sleeping bags. I don't know what to say. Kaleen is speechless as well.

Brandon laughs. 'I told him you girls wouldn't like it. But he insisted. I think all the women in Holland must be way fragile.'

Now Willem laughs. 'Don't be believing our ladies are what you say, fragile. In Nederlands, some of de tallest women. You would not be saying as much to Dutch women's faces. I tink not.' And he laughs again.

His laugh is as chocolate as his words. And it's strange, but Brandon doesn't look as attractive to me as he did a few minutes ago.

I've heard about the Dutch and their liberal ways, but somehow I can't believe Willem means to sleep with us. Not that there's room in Kaleen's tent. Anyway, right now Spirit and Watson are our first priority.

Brandon has brought some rope, which we tighten up between the trees and the fence. It's not totally ideal, but we can take turns watching the horses throughout the night. They do look pretty tired, so they'll probably sleep for most of it.

It's not bad here. There's a picnic table and a tap and trees for us to go behind too, thank goodness.

We chop up a bag of carrots and mix it with the remaining feed. The horses seem happy as long as there's something to eat. I brush out all the shed dirt from Spirit's coat and groom Watson as well, while Kaleen sets up our tent and unpacks our clothes for tomorrow and our meeting with Tarrant Moselle. She drapes our good tops and jeans over the backs of the fold-up chairs, to hang out the creases.

The guys set up their tent opposite ours, with the horses in between. I'm almost too tired to eat. I certainly don't feel like our cans of stew.

Brandon goes off on his bike and comes back half an hour later with fish and chips and ice cream for after. None of us have trouble finishing it off.

Kaleen has been very quiet. I'm not sure if it's because she's nervous being around Brandon, or angry because we've accepted help.

Willem makes us a cup of coffee and we sit at the picnic table, which is covered with crumbs of chips and ice cream wrappers.

Finally Kaleen speaks. 'I'll do the dishes,' she says, with a slight smile. She sweeps the crumbs to the ground, picks up the wrappers and takes them over to the bin. When she returns, it's like her words are a flowing highway with no end. She tells the guys everything that's happened.

Willem sits up straighter and leans forward when she mentions the snake. 'Oh, we only have de venomous vipers in de Nederlands,' he says. Then when he sees our faces, he seems to realise what he's said. 'Sounds worse den it is. Not many. Mostly we have little snakes. Grass snakes. Wid de small black band around de necks.'

'This was a brown snake. Extremely venomous,' I say, my brows furrowing. 'If you're bitten, you only have about twenty minutes to get help.'

Even by torchlight I can see Willem's aura changing to a light grey.

'And dees snakes. Dees brown snakes. Are dey around here too?' He opens his hand in an arc.

Brandon chuckles. 'Yeah, sure are, man. Also drop bears, you know, our koala ones. Drop out of the trees on your head.'

Willem briefly scans the gum trees. Then he slumps back and grins. 'I have heard of dis. No drop bears. You Ozzies trying to fool us foreigners. Anyway,' his tone becomes serious once more, 'Velvet and Kaleen have de problem. Bloody dangerous men.' Then he snorts. 'Bloody cowards are not men. More like fucking snakes den fucking snakes.'

We almost fall off our chairs laughing, not at Willem, only at what he's said. His English is pretty good really, but his swearing is perfect.

We work out a roster for watching the horses. Two hours on for each of us. Willem insists he starts the shift, and for three hours, so we ladies can get some sleep first.

I wake up through the night and can't drift off again. I glance over at Kaleen. She's breathing in the familiar way she does when she's dreaming. I check the time. It's nearly my turn to watch the horses. I cancel my alarm. It's not worth trying to get back to sleep.

I emerge from the tent, rubbing my face. Spirit and Watson are standing with their eyes closed. So it is true, horses can sleep standing up.

Willem looks at me from over his chin, which is resting on his chest. He quickly stands in a kind of salute, then sits down again.

I gasp. His aura is a prism of tiny rainbows, each colour distinct from the other, and some in hues I've never seen before. I can't move or speak.

He smiles and scrutinises his wrist. 'Hi, Velvet. Not yet your time to be watching.'

Finally my legs work, but I'm still mute. I bring over one of our chairs and sit down facing him. I'm careful not to lean back on our clothes.

Willem rises, places his jacket around my shoulders and sits once more, staring at me. For several more minutes, we're silent. Then we both talk at once, cancelling any sense.

'Ladies first. You speak, Velvet,' he says, waving his hand at me like a wand.

'How did you learn to speak English so well?' I curl a strand of my hair around my fingers. Try and face the colours shimmering before me. There's warmth emanating from him too, as soft as my name.

'We Dutch learn it at school, but still we have trouble wid de tee aitches. Just like dat.' He chuckles.

Spirit nickers softly to me and I have an excuse to get away. I find the other bag of carrots, open it and hand him one over the rope. Watson wakes and stretches out his nose in expectancy. I get a couple more of the treats and throw them onto the grass. Both horses amble after them. I notice they've knocked over their buckets of water, so I fill those up too. As I'm carrying them back from the tap, Willem comes over and takes them from me. Our hands touch with the changeover and I feel an even stronger tingle than the one I'd felt earlier. Something is definitely happening and I have no idea what.

'You love dees horses very much, I see.' He pulls on the rope fence and tightens the knots. 'I have a hound, Kelsie, at home in de Nederlands, she and I have de knowing as well.'

I only manage to nod. We're so close I feel his breath and can smell his maleness. He's more than a head taller than me, leans down when he speaks.

'In Holland when we like a lady we show it. So, Velvet, may I?'

I lift my face in answer. His lips brush my cheek and then fully to my mouth. He takes my hands in his and gazes into my eyes. I'm falling into jewelled depths, the portals of his very soul.

For the whole of my two hours' watch, we sit, hold hands and talk. It's interrupted often by kissing. I've been kissed by guys before, but never like this. It travels to my core and way beyond, to places I have only lately become more aware of.

It doesn't seem long before I hear an alarm going off.

Within minutes, Brandon is pulling open his tent. He doesn't appear surprised to see us both together. 'You better get some shut eye, man,' he says to Willem. Then he winks at me. 'Sleeping bag's still warm if you two want to borrow it.'

I feel an urge stronger than hunger, but before I can say anything Willem's soft-punched Brandon in the shoulder. Brandon pushes him back and both guys laugh.

Willem touches my chin, lifts my face to his and gives me one more long kiss before turning his back and disappearing into their tent. I have to stop myself from following.

Kaleen comes out of our tent as I'm going in.

'It's not your turn yet, Kaleen,' I say, holding open the flap.

She smiles, lifts a finger to her lips and her voice is husky. 'I know, Vel. I know. See you in the morning.'

I don't think I'm going to be able to sleep. I can hear Brandon and Kaleen talking in whispers and the horses stamping and snorting. I close my eyes, see all those wondrous colours which are Willem. I sigh and try to concentrate on a particular vibrant blue the same hue as his eyes.

I wake in a start, to a face peering in. It's Willem. 'Velvet,' he says, his voice high. 'Come and see.'

A reddish glow fills the tent. I rise, follow him outside. It's dawn and a clean red sun is rising, branding the sky in layered lines of gold and scarlet. I draw in a breath, and Kaleen and Brandon, and Willem and I, greet the morning, toasting it in with our first cup of coffee of the day.

Later, we watch the guys riding away. Willem looks back at me and waves. I almost feel like crying, but I'll see him at school tomorrow. I'm not sure I like feeling like this. Sort of out of control but not worried about it. Floaty, dreamy. OMG! It can't be, can it?

Kaleen squints into my face after I haven't answered her for the third time. 'Geez, Vel.' She pauses, stares harder. 'I think you're in love. You should see the pupils of your eyes. Way dilated. I've been doing research for my new novel about what happens when you fall in love. Apparently, the brain gives out a chemical like a drug. Oh, blurry heck, girl, you got it bad.'

In defence, I scan her eyes too. But they look no different, damn it. 'No, I haven't,' I say without conviction. I shrug and turn away to put the kettle into my backpack.

Kaleen talks slowly to me like she might to a two-year-old. 'First you got to empty it, Vel, sweetie.'

I quickly tip out the rest of the water and shove the kettle into the pack, base upwards.

We wash ourselves under the tap. Because we forgot to bring a mirror, I do Kaleen's make-up and she does mine. It's just basic lippy and mascara so it doesn't take long. Our clothes have hung out straight and look fine. We brush our hair and tie it back. More professional that way, Kaleen tells me.

'I can't believe we're actually meeting Tarrant Moselle at last,' Kaleen says, flicking some horsehair from her black top. Her voice sounds a little quivery.

I'd feel nervous as well but I'm too high on the love cloud to worry. I hope my ability is still working. Something's bothering me, though, something I've just thought of. 'Kaleen, how come you don't have to have parental permission? I mean, you are a minor. How can you sign this contract anyway?'

Kaleen turns her face away.

Now I do feel something akin to anxiety. 'You haven't told him your age, have you?'

Kaleen's silence is my answer.

I get out the make-up again. 'Well,' I say resignedly, 'we'd better get ourselves looking older then.'

When we've finished, I think we look twenty going on for twenty-five.

Kaleen keeps shaking her head and whistling. 'Wow, you look amazing, Vel. If I look as good as you, we've got it made.'

Spirit and Watson snort and take a step back when we go to saddle them. I tell myself it's the perfume.

We decide to leave all our gear here, behind a tree, pick it up later. We stack it carefully and camouflage it with leaves and grass.

As we ride off, we can hear the loudspeakers at the sale yards, a male voice rattling out escalating numbers. The auctions have begun already.

Kaleen consults her map and it's not long before we're facing a large white brick hotel with The Best Arms, in black metal print, hanging over its door. There are tables and chairs out the front, shaded by black and white umbrellas. Boxes of bright geraniums in common red, on either side of the entrance, are the hotel's only concession to colour.

'We're a tad early,' Kaleen says. She gets out her iPhone. 'I'll give Tarrant a buzz, let him know we've arrived safely.'

I dismount, lead Spirit off the road and sit down at one of the chairs. It's a lovely day for alfresco. Kaleen, with her iPhone to her ear, does the same.

Watson immediately disgraces himself. 'Shit,' I say.

'I think he has already, Vel.' Kaleen laughs. 'I'll go and get a shovel,' she says, as she hands me his reins.


We order two skinny flat whites and some double choc-chip muffins with cream. A bit of a contradiction in calories, but we like the compromise.

The sun is warming and the horses shut their eyes and alternately rest each hind leg. They look like they've lost a bit of weight, and the way my jeans feel, I have too. Kaleen was pleased when her usually super-tight best jeans were not quite as restrictive as she put them on this morning. She didn't even have to lie flat on her back to do up the zip. All right for us to have dropped some kilos, not so good for the horses, although we did have them in show condition to start with. We'll have a lot of grazing breaks on the way home, and when we get there, give them an extra large dinner.

A silver sports car convertible purrs into the hotel's car park. Kaleen sits up straighter and I do the same. We briefly stand when a shortish man, with chestnut quaffed hair and matching moustache (he must have shaved off his beard), prances up and offers us his hand. He's stylishly dressed, white chinos, light blue shirt and a yellow cardigan draped over his shoulders. A long-lens camera hangs around his neck.

'Kaleen Pingelly?' he says, scanning us both in quick succession.

Kaleen owns up to her name and they graze fingers in a missed coupling.

'And I'm Velvet Brown. Kaleen's agent,' I say, grasping his hand firmly and shaking it in what I hope is a convincingly professional manner.

'Nice to meet you both. I'm sure.' He sits down, retrieves a silver curlicued clipboard from his man-bag and places it on the table. After ordering a macchiato, he leans back, arms folded and mouth clamped shut. His eyes keep darting from Kaleen to me.

I crack the silence. Bring up percentages, ISBN numbers, cover art and things I've researched on the internet about 'being an agent'.

His answers are perfunctory. I'm becoming disturbed about his niggling shadow, not quite forming to monsterish but looking, the longer we go on, like a Category Four.

As I've said before, if you have to meet a monster, a Category Four is the least dangerous. But like Dad and Danny, who are very pale Category Fours, they can be annoying. Don't expect them to stick up for you. They easily take the side of least resistance and hate confrontation.

In another hiatus of silence, Kaleen says she has to go the Ladies.

Tarrant offers to hold the horses for us, so we hand him the reins and scoot off.

'So, Vel, what do you think?' Kaleen says, through closed lips, once we're in the relative seclusion of the toilets.

I can't tell her right away. I'm forming my answer, wanting it to come out right. I don't want to smash her hopes.

Kaleen grabs me by the shoulders and shakes me. Then she slumps back against the sink. 'Oh no! He's not a monster, is he?' She grabs me again. 'Vel, talk to me.'

'Not really. Not properly.' Suddenly I need to go. I hurry into a cubicle and close the door.

Kaleen bangs on it. 'Just tell me, Vel. I have to know. He seems quite nice to me. A bit gay actually, if anything. And they're usually okay.'

I tell her what I've seen.

'Oh, a Category Four, Vel. That's the head in the sand one, isn't it?'

I come out and wash my hands. I'm pleased they have soap and paper hand towels. I hate those hand dryers.

'Yeah, and he's not really what I'd call a confirmed one. Seems to be morphing in and out. Probably having a conflict of interest.'

Kaleen hugs me. 'Well,' she says, smiling. 'That's okay then. Let's go back out and sign the deal.'

'Sure,' I say. 'That's if he still wants to. I think signing the deal may be what his conflict of interest is about. I'm not sure he's convinced about our age. Anyway, I thought you were using your age as a spin for a publisher to market you on?'

Kaleen looks at the floor, nudges a dropped piece of paper towel towards the bin with the toe of her boot. 'It wasn't working. I haven't told you, Vel, but except for the Canadian publisher, I've had dozens of rejections. Then, as soon as I didn't mention I was fourteen, Wanda-Willow Press wanted me.'

I look directly at her. 'You should have left the contacting to me, Kaleen. That's what you have an agent for.'

All goes well. The publican agrees to be another signatory to the contract, doesn't bat a moustache hair at us. I reckon we could have easily ordered a bottle of wine with no questions asked. For a fraction of a second, I ponder on doing just that. But lack of money, and the feeling I don't want to push our luck, prevent me.

We toast the book contract in with coffee, the same as we had done earlier to the stunning sunrise.

<h1 style="text-align:center">25</h1>

We return to the truck stop, hold our breath that our gear will still be there, and let it out with synchronised sighs when we see it is. We give the horses a whole bag of carrots between them and let them have an hour of roadside grazing.

Now that we're heading home, I feel relieved. Things could have been worse, much worse.

Kaleen is taking us back a different route. It's a bit longer, but off the main highway until about the last twenty-five kilometres. Hopefully, this way we'll avoid any danger. I think of those men in the SUV and shiver despite the warming sun.

'Well, that was ace, wasn't it, Vel? The best quest since *The Hobbit*!'

Kaleen's smiling and flicking her long reins about. Watson's ears are wobbling from side to side listening, and both horses are definitely stepping out in a faster walk than they have for the entire ride.

I gulp back a breath. She's done it again, pre-empted fate. We're not home yet. I flick my reins gently across Spirit's rump.

'I wonder why Tarrant didn't take any pics, Kaleen. He had his camera.'

We ride on in silence. I think we both know why he hadn't. He was protecting himself. If push came to shove, I'm betting he wouldn't even acknowledge meeting us. Although we did have the publican as a witness. Still, witnesses can be bought off. And Kaleen's Tarrant Moselle, if indeed that was his name, looked to be from a top paddock and very well shod, so he certainly could afford it.

I'm chuckling about this metaphor when Kaleen pulls up and takes out her map again. (She refuses to use GPS. It's not in her Quest ethics of hardship.)

'We need to turn, just up ahead, I think,' she says.

A hare dashes across our path and the horses falter a step.

'At least that wasn't a black cat.' I grin.

Kaleen glares at me and I wonder why she didn't laugh. Maybe she's not as sure of herself as she's trying to make out.

We take a couple of wrong turns and end up letting the horses have some more verge side grass. There's no source of water this way and I'm getting concerned. Kaleen's face is as red as fire and the afternoon promises to be a hotter one than yesterday. Tipped to reach 36 degrees Celsius. Mum would say that was nearly a century in her day, before metric. It's times like these, I'm thankful for my Aboriginal inheritance. I don't feel the heat as much as Kaleen, and I never have trouble with sunburn. We also forgot to fill our water bottles. Now there's only a half-full one left between us.

Two riding hours later and we've finished that bottle. But at least Kaleen's sat nav (which she's finally decided to use) indicates we're going the right way, thank god. It's also good that Willem and Brandon took back some more of our gear, as well as our tent and sleeping bags. And without the horse feed too, our backpacks are way lighter. We left the tins of stew, and some of our other food, back at the truck stop as a sort of payment for our outdoor lodgings.

I'd read Robert Louis Stevenson did something like this when he trekked across France with his donkey. His travel book must have been where I got the idea about a quest and a donkey. It wasn't in the *Lord of the Rings*. I make a promise to myself to read those books as soon as I can.

We find a farmhouse and a very nice lady farmer shows us where the cattle trough is. After a short rest to cool down, the horses have a long drink.

She brings us wet facecloths, gives us tall glasses of homemade lemonade and freshly baked cookies and we sit and enjoy them beneath an apple tree. It has no fruit on it, or under it, and I'm guessing it's all in apple pies in the freezer.

Back on the road again with bottles full of real orange cordial (it even has the pith) and pockets full of biscuits (so much for losing any more weight), Kaleen seems more positive, chatting away to me or Watson and making silly jokes.

Pushing into a working trot, we stop an hour later and, when the sun shines directly above us, we get off and let the horses graze under some willow trees. We wait until four o'clock before setting off again. Despite the setbacks, we've made heaps good time.

As the day goes on, the sun sneaks behind some clouds and the air feels thundery. The horses are zooming along now; it's hard to stop them cantering. It's so much cooler and we're so close to Brandon's, I almost imagine I can hear Ganymede and Topper neighing out to us.

Back onto the highway, twenty-five kilometres to go. Then we'll be home. At every one of the hills, we dismount and walk the horses up. They must be tired, though they're not showing it.

Another hour later, we're trotting fast along a flat stretch of highway when we see a cop car coming towards us. It's not doing the speed limit as it drives past. It's going much slower.

Kaleen reins in Watson and we drop back to a walk alongside each other. She nudges me with an extended elbow. 'What's a bet he's looking for us?' she says, and laughs.

This time I'm not laughing. I can see the car doing a U-turn a little way down the road. Now it's heading straight for us, with its blue light flashing and siren whooping. Bloody hell, it seems even some police know nothing about horses. It's good that ours are mega-quiet. Rushing up making so much noise is like an attack, even worse than sneaking up.

Watson and Spirit watch, heads cocked, with quizzical looks like dogs, as the car comes up and the driver's side window glides down.

'Kaleen Pingelly? Velvet Brown?'

For a second, I'm transported back to this morning and our meeting with Tarrant Moselle. But this voice is not accommodating, although it is strangely familiar.

Kaleen grabs my arm. 'I know that voice,' she whispers in a hiss. 'It's one of the men who were outside the shed yesterday, at the abandoned house.'

'I'm Sergeant Brannigan. As of this morning, you've been reported as missing persons. Can you step off the horses, please?' the cop says, as his sidekick gets out of the car.

God, next he'll be asking us to put our hands behind our heads and lean against the horses' rumps.

Kaleen, who has no Category Four traits like fear of confrontation, asks bluntly, 'Was it you two yesterday, in the SUV?'

The sidekick, who announces himself as Sergeant Farrelli, answers her. His accent and words confirm what suspicion indicated.

They take our backpacks and tell us to go directly home, no detours.

'Get those horses moving. Don't spare the hooves. And don't slow down until you're home.' Sergeant Brannigan's exact words as we rode off.

'Geez, Vel, Absolutely no idea about horses,' Kaleen says, as we canter off down the verge. 'They could learn a lot from their mounted police division. And yesterday, in that SUV with the weird bull-bar, how were we supposed to know they were undercover cops?'

I cough. 'I guess tearing towards us with headlights flashing means Stop in police books. Maybe they didn't think how it looked to us. That SUV was bloody terrifying.'

When we can't see the police car any more, we drop back to a walk. There's another hill coming up.

'What strikes me as strange, Kaleen, is they got the missing person report this morning and yet they were tailing us yesterday. Something doesn't add up.'

'Blurry heck, Vel, and now they've got all the details of my novel. The signed copies of my book deal and everything.'

'Well,' I say smiling faintly. 'That's one good thing. Tarrant can't wiggle out of it now.'

I'm about to ask what we're going to tell Brandon and Willem about picking up Ganny and Topper, when we see the guys on their racing bikes, with their peloton of riders, skimming towards us. Once more they're out in front. Willem sees us first and waves before he even gets close.

As they pass, Brandon shakes a hand at Kaleen. He's talking so loudly to Willem I can hear him as if he was next to me. 'God, man. You call that a Category Two? Bloody Dutch. No idea.'

Their conjoined, long laughter trails back like an insult. Oh, my god, what has Kaleen told them? I glare at her. She's looking at the nails of one of her hands, like she hasn't heard a thing. Or doesn't want me to know she has.

'I'll give the guys a text when we get home, tell them we'll pick the horses up tomorrow. That's if I'm not grounded,' Kaleen says, biting off a piece of nail.

My words die in my mouth. So what if Kaleen has told them about my ability? They have no right to make fun of it. But her silence is worse than any confession. My stomach is heavy and the thrill of seeing Willem again is now plummeting with my heart. More than anything I want to go home, get this damned quest over with.

As we go downhill, I push Spirit into a canter and when I look back Watson and Kaleen are way behind us.

When we finally ride up Kaleen's driveway, we see the flashing lights of the cop car near her house and there, holding tightly to each other, are Dad with Mum, and Mr Pingelly with Mrs Pingelly. They let go of each other and rush towards us.

## 26

I'm grounded indefinitely. I don't know when I'll see Spirit again. Kaleen and I have been forbidden to see each other for ever. And I have Danny's duties around the farm for the rest of the year. Mum and Dad have even taken away my iPhone and laptop. I'm not sure how they'll stop Kaleen and me from seeing each other, though.

I'm still angry with Kaleen, so I don't sit with her on the bus even though she's looking as excited as a seal at feeding time. I also ignore Willem and Brandon at recess break.

Why did Kaleen have to tell them? What did I do to deserve to be treated like this? My life matters, and I can't help having this weird ability, or falling in love. Amazingly awesome as that feeling has been, its downfall is, in equal measure, completely devastating. Perhaps I should tell Kaleen to write this down in her clues folder under a new title: 'Love Chemical Withdrawals'.

And I can't believe Willem would make fun of me, laughing like that. Practically in front of my face too. He seemed such a nice guy. And what if he tells everyone? It's bad enough being called Half-caste, like I'm incomplete somehow.

At lunchtime, a much-subdued Kaleen sits down carefully next to me. I shrug her arm away when she tries to put it around my shoulders.

'Come on, Vel, what is it? This can't be because we're not supposed to be talking to each other. You were so happy before. Did you and Willem have a fight? Have I done something? I mean, I'm sorry about the quest going wrong, but how was I supposed to know Dwayne would tell on us? He says he didn't mean to of course. And actually I believe him. He's so dozy in love with Coral Lee.' Kaleen stops and stares at me. 'Vel, you're

149

angry at me, aren't you? Oh, blurryheck.' She runs the words together, 'Tell me! What have I done?'

I take a deep breath, and without meeting her eyes I tell her about Brandon and ask if she heard what he said as they were riding past us yesterday.

'Yes,' she says slowly. 'About the Category Two. I think they were arguing. In Holland, it's all really flat, not many hills and what Willem was calling a Category Two…' She stops, looks at me again and shrieks. 'Oh, sheez, Vel! Now I know why you're so cross. I swear to gosh, I never told them anything. The category thing: they're gradients in cycling. The steepness of hills. It's what they call them. Nothing to do with your categories. Just the degree of difficulty.'

I feel all kinds of foolish. Come to think of it, I do recall Danny going on about something like categories when he and Dad were watching the Tour de France last year.

Kaleen hugs me tightly and I hug her back.

'Come on,' she says, her tone rising to cheeky. 'Let's get out of here. Go to Caz's café. Skinny lattes are on me.'

As we're about to enter the shop, Willem comes up alongside on his bike. 'Dis afternoon I am having a student-free,' he says, dismounting. He holds open the door of the café, 'Ladies, could it be my treat? Velvet, I want to talk. You seem to be upsetting about someting.'

Kaleen smiles at me, and then squeezes my arm. 'I've just remembered.' She turns to Willem. 'I've got stuff to do. Can I have a rain check?'

Willem looks concerned. 'What is dis rain check?' he says, as we enter the café.

I take his hand. 'I'll tell you in a minute. Willem, right now I could kill for a coffee.'

We sit at the back of the café in a little booth. It has high wooden sides and soft padded cushions. Willem tips my face up to his and our kiss seems to go on forever.

I can't tell him what's been bothering me as it would mean I'd have to disclose my monster sight. It's too early for that. I tell him I'm upset about not being able to see Spirit any more and how I've been grounded until eternity, or, I guess, when I'm twenty-one. Whichever comes first.

He chuckles over this. Then he holds my hand and kisses open my fingers with his mouth. 'When parents make impossible rules, it is easier for dem to break, so I would not be worrying. Here, I will cheer you up.' He places a little yellow and white gift-wrapped box into my open palm.

It's then I notice his knuckles are calloused.

'Willem, what's happened to your hands?'

He glances at his knuckles like he's seeing them for the first time. 'Oh, dat is not any trouble. Dat is from boxing. I do it back home in de Nederlands. For fun.'

I open the box. Nestled inside is a small gold pendant on a gold chain, in the shape of a sun. Inside the sun is some white hair twined into a horseshoe shape and interlaced with silky blue ribbon.

'Spirit's hair from de mane. I get it from him when I was on watch. I have my Swiss army knife scissors, so I do not hurt.' Willem takes the necklace from me, puts it around my neck and does up the clasp. 'De sun it is a reminder of our first sunrise. One of many more, I am hoping. And now you will wear Spirit close to your heart. Where I would want to be also.' He touches my chest and my heart leaps.

I'm breathless. 'Oh, Willem, I love it! Thanks so much. It's the most beautiful, thoughtful present anyone has ever given me!'

Willem kisses me again and from the corners of my half-closed eyes I see the waitress placing down our coffees. She's smiling, but says nothing.

I know Kaleen would think Willem way lame saying what he did about being near my heart. But she can't see his aura. The clarity and trueness of its colours.

We sit quietly for many minutes. Our eyes tell each other all we need to know. I am found and lost in his. That wonderful blue. I realise it's the same colour as the ribbon in my pendant.

'Velvet, I am to be going home soon. My exchange is running out. And if you are to be grounded forever...' He stops and winks. 'But seriously, Velvet. We must be keeping dis. What we have.'

'There's Facebook.' Now who's sounding lame?

'Skype is better.' Willem kisses me again. 'We can talk and see ourselfs. And I will be coming again in January. You will be meeting my parents.'

I marvel at our different cultures. In Australia, guys shy away from stuff like this.

Our coffees stay untouched. The bell has rung and I have to get back to school.

The rest of the week goes by in a dream. Every lunchtime, Willem and I go to Caz's Café and order coffee. Sometimes we manage to finish it, sometimes we don't. I'm worried about Kaleen, though. She hasn't been at school and without my iPhone I can't ring her. And with Mum and Dad watching me like tigers, I can't even call her on the landline.

## 27

Kaleen's back at school the following Monday, extra tanned and looking as happy as Spirit and Watson did with the fallen apples. It turns out she's been on a quick holiday with her parents, to Hawaii of all places.

'Mother and Father have made up,' she tells me over recess, her cheeks glowing. 'Donovan's not coming back.'

I feel the warmth drain from my face.

'Not like Chocka and Jim, Vel, don't worry. Donovan rang me while we were in Hawaii. Told me he's sorry for what happened with Mother. He wished us all the best of luck with the horses. He also asked if I could keep Ganymede, but not to tell anyone he rang, so keep it quiet.'

'That's wonderful, Kaleen. I mean, about your parents making up.' I take out my vanilla square, make indents in the icing with my finger.

'Geez, Vel, you don't look too pleased to me.'

'I am, Kaleen. It's just I haven't been thinking about Jim and Chocka lately. I've been so happy. And you saying about them now made me remember.' I wipe my hands on my paper serviette. 'There's been nothing on the news. Do you know what's going on?'

Kaleen rubs her chin. 'Long story. You having lunch again with Willem?'

I nod. 'It's his last day,' I say, a knot in my throat.

Kaleen gives me a long hug. 'I'll tell you all about it on the way home then. On the bus.'

Kaleen's not on the bus and when I get home Mum waves to me as I come in. She has the phone to her ear and is nodding and saying 'Yes' and 'Oh'. She mouths the word 'Kaleen' and hands the receiver to me.

'Hi, Vel. Sorry I wasn't on the bus,' Kaleen says, her tone apologetic.

'Parentals are into the happy family stage. Wanted to take me shopping. I'm not complaining. I got heaps of cool gear.'

I think to myself, Yes, that'd be right. Kaleen gets a holiday and nice stuff while I get impossible punishment. I so miss Spirit. I ask Kaleen how he's doing.

'Oh, he's fine. Listen, Vel, I'm coming over soon. Father will drop me off at your place in about an hour. Then we can talk.'

I'm about to ask, 'What about us being forbidden to see each other?' but she's already hung up.

Mum hands me my iPhone as I put down the landline one. 'You can have this back now, Velvet,' she says. 'Kaleen and I had a lovely chat. She's made me understand it was more her fault you both going away to Adelaide on the horses like that. Although with what she's been going through lately, you can hardly blame her for wanting to get away. Isn't it great news about her folks, though? And so wonderful that the police have got the killers.'

So they have found them.

I look at my iPhone like it's gold. I touch my pendant, think of how I won't be seeing Willem again until the new year. I feel happy and sad at the same time. Kaleen would write that up as melancholy.

Kaleen arrives within the hour and we go up to my room. Mum brings us hot chocolate with marshmallows, like she has before. I notice Kaleen's chocolate has way more marshmallows in it than mine.

We lie back on my bed. I pull down my clown doll and sit him on my chest.

Kaleen has her hands behind her head. 'I'm going to do what's called a monologue now, Vel,' she says.

'I bloody well know what a monologue is, Kaleen. I do English lit. too, remember.'

'Well, Vel, I want to make sure you don't interrupt.'

'I'm not promising that. But go ahead anyway.'

Kaleen stretches out a finger and touches my clown doll's nose. 'Well, we got back from Hawaii on Saturday morning. After lunch, I overheard

Mother telling J.D. Claridge to come over Sunday afternoon. So I got prepared.'

'How do you prepare for that?'

Kaleen glares at me. 'I'm getting to it. When Mother was planning to leave Father, she had a big clean-out of the attic.'

'Hang on, Kaleen. You never told me about your Mother wanting to leave.'

Kaleen rolls her eyes. 'Are you going to let me get on with this or not?'

I close my lips tightly.

Kaleen smiles and continues, 'Well, I found my nursery intercom thing. To get to the point, Saturday night, when everyone was asleep, I taped it onto the bottom of the dining table. I had the listening part in my room.'

Kaleen stops, sips her chocolate and scoops up a marshmallow with her tongue.

'It was a bit crackly even though I'd put in new batteries. I could still hear them though. I mean, Mother's softly spoken but JD doesn't hold back. Quite a voice. It seems like those plain clothes cops we saw on Saturday had been onto a new lead in Adelaide. Think about it, Vel. Donovan goes off on a horse and then, a few days later, we're heading off on horses too.'

'We might have just been going for a ride.'

'Not with all that gear. And when Old Ma Izzy told JD about the scent trail leading from our place to the bodies, and then JD told the detectives, everyone was under suspicion.'

I snatch a short gasp of breath.

'Not us killing them, silly, but I guess they wondered what we were up to. Maybe meeting Donovan or something. Probably thought we might have been in danger.'

I take a long swig of my chocolate. My marshmallows have melted and it's extra sweet. 'So that's what the cop meant about babysitting us. I thought he was referring to our age.'

Kaleen snorts. 'He sort of was. Anyway, the other cop, the one with the accent, turns out to be a plant, an undercover agent.'

'On the cops' side, though?'

'Yeah, of course.' Kaleen's voice rises slightly.

'Who did he infiltrate? The Jugular Jackals bikie gang?'

'Nope, much further from home. Well, the parent company is. Or should I say Family.' Kaleen chuckles. 'They have flourishing ones here in Australia too. And in nearly every country in the world, if their reputation is to be believed.'

'Family?'

'The Family.' Kaleen sighs with exaggeration. 'You know, Vel, Mafia. I was right about that cop's accent. He is Italian.'

I sit up and put back my clown doll. I feel I have more questions than when I started. But the picture has cleared a bit.

'It's like this, Vel,' Kaleen continues after draining her cup. 'The cops even suspected Father at first. And when the affair came out, about Mother and Donovan, well, you can imagine what that looked like.'

When I remain silent, Kaleen peers at me, her eyes hooded. 'Come on, Vel. Think laterally.'

My mind is on speed dial. Italians? Mafia? Italian undercover policeman? Jim and Chocka murdered? Chocka, Mafia? And then I try and recall Chocka's last name. Distinctly Italian. He must have been given the kiss of death. That's what Mafia do to their own when they're pissed off with them, isn't it? Seems like he'd made a far worse enemy than Mr Pingelly. And even the bikie gang knew there was a contract out on him. Poor Jim had been collateral damage.

I close my eyes in a long blink and then in my mind, just like the Freya poem except not in writing, I hear his real name. 'Concertichocka Saltarelli,' I say.

Kaleen pats my shoulder like she's giving me the stamp of approval. Then her eyes open wide. 'How the bleary heck did you remember his name?'

I look directly into Kaleen's eyes, note the flecks of gold. Gold seems to be featuring a lot lately. Good omen? 'I must have remembered it subliminally, like I did Old Ma Izzy's poem. Chocka said he was from

Croatia. But his surname sounded more Italian to me. I was suspicious back then. But when he was killed, I forgot all about it, until now.'

'Death does not make innocence. Being in the Mafia, Chocka's probably murdered heaps of people,' Kaleen says, spreading her arms wide.

Suddenly she screams, jumps up and claps her hands. I stare at her like she's gone mad.

'That will be the new title for my old novel, Vel! *Death Does Not Innocence Make*. What do you think?'

'Wonderful, Kaleen. Wonderful! Much better than *Bitter the Taste of Murder*.'

## 28

When Mr Pingelly arrives to take Kaleen home, I notice something missing. His Category One shadow jagging has all but disappeared. And his aura is glowing with little golden highlights.

I'm so happy I wasn't right about him being guilty of the murders. Like Old Ma Izzy had said on my first visit to her place, when I'd made so many wrong assumptions, 'Now, Velvet. Don't be worrying none. 'Tis normal to get things incorrect sometimes.'

I'm pleased Kaleen is on the bus the next morning. There are a few questions tangled in my mind, which I need to straighten out.

Unfortunately, somehow Spider Johnson has been allowed back on and is making up for lost travel. Every time Mr Tangelo stops the bus, we have to stop talking because without the noise of the engine, everyone can hear us.

When the bus is rolling again, I tell Kaleen I'm not grounded any more. And I give her a high five for having that chat with Mum.

'No worries, Vel.'

'I still have to do all of Danny's chores for the next two months, though,' I say. 'But it's great I'm free again. I can even come over tonight and we can go for a ride. I can't wait to see Spirit. I'm bringing him a whole bag of apples!'

The bus stops and we slide into silence. We sit smiling at each other and inwardly willing Spider Johnson to shut his bloody mouth, which he does eventually and the bus lumbers up the gears once more into a noisy backdrop.

'One thing I'm not sure of, Kaleen, is how Donovan figures in all this. Why was he under suspicion at all? He had no motive. Jim and Chocka were no threat to him. They certainly weren't after your mother. I mean, I know you thought Jim was involved with her, but you were wrong.'

'Yeah, I was, Vel. There's no doubt that Chocka and Jim were gay and wonderfully in love. You can't fake things like that.'

'So, what's the story? Was Donovan totally innocent, then?'

'Well, Vel, not totally. I mean, he didn't murder anyone.' Kaleen clears her throat. 'There's been nothing officially said, but I think Donovan set up the scent trail a few days after the bodies were discovered. Remember how I found Jim's hat in the stockmen's quarters, in Donovan's room? Donovan must have used it, dragged it along the ground. Probably did it off Cody.'

A yell from near the front heralds another stop. Spider Johnson's hanging out of the window and swearing at a passing car. Even having to sit at the front of the bus, near Mr Tangelo, hasn't deterred him. He's laughing, and OMG, now he's pulled down his jeans and is flashing the new Year Eight girls with a brown eye. The silly things are giggling at him too. We'll be getting to school at lunchtime at this rate. Oh well, I don't really care. No Willem to share lunch with today. I look at Kaleen and I feel a little guilty for feeling like this. She's smiling and glowing like her father. She's such a great friend, I should be happy for her.

I'm nearly asleep before the bus moves again. Kaleen nudges me.

I sit up straight, jolt my brain into thinking. 'So, Kaleen, why would Donovan do that? Set up a false trail, I mean?'

Kaleen sighs again, but it's a light-hearted one. 'To pin the murder on Father, of course. Father had the motive. Father and Chocka didn't get along very well. Chocka was the union rep, remember? And with all that trouble earlier at Father's business – strikes and everything – to quote the detectives, Father was "a person of interest". Donovan knew that.'

I'm almost about to ask, 'Why would Donovan bother?' And then I get it. These love chemicals do make you dozy at times. For a second, I feel sorry for Dwayne. 'Oh, I understand now. With your father out of the picture, Donovan would have had your mother all to himself.'

Kaleen grimaces. 'You're right, Vel. You know, I really did mind about their affair. I guess Donovan isn't a bad guy. Remember he did save Ganymede from that dreadful horse stud. And Father did turn mean back there for a while. When he was under all that pressure at work, he was horrible to Mother. I didn't blame her, but I still didn't like what was going on with her and Donovan.'

If only Kaleen knew. She doesn't know the half of it. I'm so glad I didn't tell her about her father turning into a Category One. He's fine now, so I'll never have to.

Kaleen continues, 'Terrible thing to do, though. Trying to make it look like Father killed Jim and Chocka. And it nearly backfired on Donovan too. The detectives found the scent trail led back to the stockmen's quarters and when Donovan did a runner they got really suspicious.'

'Why did he run? Or ride, more to the point?'

'He and Mother had broken up. Father had given Mother an ultimatum: Donovan or him. That's what the big argument was about before we went TAOB.  Mother chose Father. So Donovan cleared out. It's awesome at home now. And Father has been heaps nice over the past week.'

The bus stops in a skid. Spider Johnson's impersonating Mick Jagger, he's on his knees in the aisle, air guitar, the works. I have to admit he is kind of funny. I try not to smile. I don't want to encourage him.

Now the bus has stopped, everyone on board is murmuring low, not wanting to be heard. Everyone except Spider Johnson, who's now doing a terrible rendition of 'I Can't Get No Satisfaction'.

Kaleen sits up, a gleam in her eye. Her voice stretches loud along the whole length of the bus, catching Spider Johnson in mid-sentence of 'And I try...' 'Mrs Islington-Prior had us over to her place for a dinner party on Sunday, Vel,' she says.

For a second, my mind scrabbles with the name, then pops it up as Old Ma Izzy.

Everyone else on the bus is silent, a collective animal breathing curiosity, wanting to hear more dirt on the Pingellys.

Instantly, I know what Kaleen is doing. Clearing her name.

For the next few minutes, we exchange conversation like air freshener. Kaleen brings up all the facts in favour of her family, recounting the table talk at the dinner party of her mother's respected friend. Everyone knows Old Ma Izzy. In a town this small, she's hard to miss.

I agree loudly with Kaleen, saying how pleased I am about the innocence of Mr Pingelly, and how wonderful it is that the murderers have been caught.

Spider Johnson is quiet and even Mr Tangelo has stopped tapping on his steering wheel. My only regret is that Kiss is not on the bus to hear it all.

As the engine clatters to life, Kaleen adds in even louder tones, 'Oh, and by the way, Vel, Mrs Islington-Prior told me her colt Zeus is ready for backing and she wants you to be the first on him. She says Indigenous people make the best riders.'

My mind catapults. Oh, damn it that Kiss isn't here!

Finally, we make it to school. Everyone else has gone in. Kiss arrives late too. Her mother gets out of their black Mercedes and walks Kiss up to the school stairs. She gives her a peck on the cheek. As I get closer, I see she's the same category as her daughter. Like I thought: born, not made. True monsters are spawned that way. Hereditary.

Kiss's mother glares at us, her face streaming venomous lines of brackish light. Proving my point, she spits into our faces. 'Little slags,' she growls, as she passes us. Even her voice is monsterish.

Kaleen catches my eye, her face asks the question. Is she?

I nod, we both smile and arm in arm we climb the steps into our future. Our friendship's so strong there's no more need for words.

*

## Journal: Tuesday 3 April

I can't put this entry into the textbook journal, as I've buried the time capsule in the garden. This is a written map to explain where the capsule is, if anything happens to me or Kaleen. Kaleen came up with an idea of how to mark where it is. It's a bit Robert Louis Stevenson Treasure Islandish in the sense that X marks the spot – black mondo grass in lines of a huge X, with the capsule buried at the point where the cross crosses. Kaleen says it's so obvious as to make it not obvious. And I know what she means.

Sebby watched us bury it. We had a little ceremony with our favourite snacks, and gave him the leftovers. Even Spirit and Watson were there too.

It's my Moment of Truth this Saturday. That's when I get on Zeus for the very first time. I'm hoping I'm up to it, but I feel way more confident, after everything that's happened this year.

When will I dig up the capsule? Kaleen says it's all up to the vagaries of time. Whatever that means.